I0819796

Joel and the Egyptian Cat

Joel and the Egyptian Cat

How Cats Came to Jerusalem

DAVID L. DUDLEY

RESOURCE *Publications* • Eugene, Oregon

JOEL AND THE EGYPTIAN CAT
How Cats Came to Jerusalem

Resource Publications
An Imprint of Wipf and Stock Publishers
199 W. 8th Ave., Suite 3
Eugene, OR 97401

www.wipfandstock.com

PAPERBACK ISBN: 978-1-6667-3338-9
HARDCOVER ISBN: 978-1-6667-2798-2
EBOOK ISBN: 978-1-6667-2799-9

JANUARY 4, 2022 8:43 AM

For Eileen, Chris, Amanda, Noah, Aaron, Joy, Daniel, Aiden, Emma, Madaline, Jack, Michael, Will, and Kay.

In honor of Jackson, Hazel, Greta, and Logan.

In affectionate memory of Ares, Kenji, Tosca, Fricka, Mary, Caleb, Calico, Joshua, Hershey, and Henry.

Especially Henry.

One

Joel was wide awake, so he peered out at the stars. The night was warm for springtime, and no refreshing breeze wafted through the loft room window. Nearby, his father snored. Joel wished his mother would rouse and get him to turn on his side, which sometimes helped. But no one moved, and the snoring went on. How anyone could sleep through such racket was a mystery. Joel knew *he* couldn't, and dawn was hours away.

Next to Joel, his sister Miriam lay lost in dreams. She often reported them in the morning, while they were still "full of colors," as she put it. Mother would ask what she dreamed about, and Miriam's answer was usually the same: "I was a princess in the palace of King Solomon, and I ate honey on bread every day and had a new tunic every week. One embroidered with lilies."

Joel dreamed, too, but not of dwelling in a palace. Instead, he imagined flying with the birds—birds as countless as the stars, even now winging their way north to unknown lands where they would nest, lay eggs, and hatch their young.

Just then, their cries resounded somewhere above Jerusalem. Not even darkness could keep the birds from seeking their summer homes. Cranes, pelicans, eagles, falcons—birds of more kinds than one could count, birds white and golden and black, birds with snakelike necks and legs like reeds—rising, diving, turning—and forever calling, urging one another to stay with the flock, to fly, fly through darkness and weariness and storms—until they came to their journeys' end in mysterious lands far from Jerusalem.

Jerusalem: city of the great King, where Joel had been born, had always lived, and would most probably spend his life until, as the old men declared, he would be gathered to his ancestors. The old men also asserted that Jerusalem, chosen by YAH to be the site of the temple from which he would rule his people, could not be moved, but would abide forever. They had to be right: what power on the earth could move Mount Zion? Surely, it was fixed. Unchanging.

Like my life, Joel thought.

The calls went on and on. Come morning, everyone in the city could look up and watch in wonder as the migrating flocks flew overhead. But now, in the darkest part of the night, perhaps he, Joel, was the only person in Jerusalem listening to their cries. Although he did not know their language—only King Solomon was said to have the power to understand the animals—Joel felt he knew what they were urging: "Come fly with us! Come fly!"

Where they went, he did not know exactly. But one thing he *did* know: he *would* join with the birds, if only he had wings and were not caught in the invisible snare everyone else called Jerusalem.

When Father roused Miriam and Joel at dawn, he realized he had slept, despite the snoring, but for how long he wasn't sure. He didn't want to get up and do the morning's chores; surely Father had wakened the family too early. Joel yanked the thin coverlet over his head, but Miriam snatched it back, complaining that he always took more than his fair part.

He pulled a short tunic over the loincloth in which he slept. His skin, light brown on his chest and thighs, was darker where the sun had tanned his face, arms, and calves. He tied leather sandals on his feet and ran his fingers through his curly black hair. His mother despaired that it was always such a mess and sometimes asked why he insisted on looking like a street beggar. Why couldn't he be neat, like his sister? Miriam smirked at that compliment, and Joel dreamed of pulling her perfect hair until she squawked. His own needed cutting badly, but until then, a cloth cap helped hide the offending tangle beneath it.

Now Mother added her voice to Father's, reminding the children of their responsibilities: a fire to start, water to be fetched from the Gihon Spring, and bread to bake. But first, Joel had to untie the family's two sheep, Laban and Dodo, and get them out the door, ready to meet his friend Issachar, whose father kept a large flock outside the city walls. His sons took turns guarding their sheep day and night. But Issachar, the youngest, still had to sleep at home, even though he begged to keep night vigil with his brothers. Issachar was thirteen, like Joel, but people joked that his mother still treated him like a child, afraid that her precious baby would be devoured by a night-hunting hungry lion. To avoid daily squabbles, Issachar's father, Jonadab, did not argue the point. The lad was allowed, at least, to drive some of the neighbors' animals out of the city and into the countryside. Most families on Joel's street owned a couple of sheep, and they paid Jonadab to look after them.

Laban and Dodo were more than eager to be untied and let outside. They knew very well what was coming, so Joel had no difficulty getting them to the door. And here came Issachar, right on time, surrounded by a small flock of other families' animals.

"Mother, Issachar's here. May I walk with him—just down to the corner?"

"Yes, but come right back. You don't want to be late for school."

Joel let the sheep join the others.

"Good morning," Issachar greeted him. "You look half asleep."

"It's how I feel. You?"

Issachar sighed. "The same as always. I wish I was coming home to sleep instead of going out. You have it easy, Joel. No matter if it's hot, cold, or raining, you go to the temple school and sit inside all day in comfort while I have to put up with these stupid, smelly animals."

Joel patted Laban's head. "You're not stupid, are you?" The sheep nuzzled his hand. "And what about you, little Dodo? You're as wise as the king himself."

Issachar scoffed. “Maybe you’re right. They’re smart enough to get us to take care of them their whole lives. That doesn’t mean that they don’t smell awful and drop their dung everywhere.”

“I know. When I get back, I’ll have to clean up after them.”

Issachar smiled. “At least that’s one thing we don’t have to put up with very often, unless we’ve got a sick or hurt animal.” His family kept no sheep on the first floor of their house, as the other families did.

The sheep were getting restless, eager to leave the city and trot into the fields, where there was plenty of grass.

“I have to hurry,” Issachar said. “Why don’t you ask your father if you can come with me sometime? The days would go faster if you were there to talk with me.”

“Father wouldn’t let me. He says that learning to be a scribe is a great blessing from YAH, and I have to study harder than any of the other boys. When I’m a man, I can get the best work and have a fine house.”

“Stop complaining, then. One day, you’ll be advisor to the king, and I’ll be ”

“What?”

“A stupid shepherd.”

Joel wanted to tell his friend that wasn’t true, but he knew it was. You followed in the steps of your father. If he was a shepherd, so would you be. If he had been trained to write and to read, so would you, even if you wanted something different. Things were as they were, as they had been since olden times. As YAH decreed. Issachar needed to accept that he’d always be a shepherd, and Joel had to understand that he’d be a scribe. Oh, if only he and Issachar could trade places! Then Joel could spend his days outside, with the wildflowers, the grasses, the fields of wheat and barley, the groves of olive and fig, and the many animals one might see: foxes, badgers, voles, mongooses—even poisonous asps. It could be dangerous—and exciting. And fun.

“I’ll come to your house this evening,” Issachar said. “Perhaps we can play senet.”

"Good. Now go and enjoy your day. And don't get eaten by a lion!"

"At least that would be something exciting!"

Joel laughed. "You two obey your master," he told Laban and Dodo. "Remember what happens to disobedient sheep."

"Roasted mutton!" Issachar threatened. "Don't worry. These two are obedient. You can tell they've been raised in a strict home. Like you!"

Joel punched his friend's arm. "May YAH protect you this day," he told Issachar.

"And you, my brother."

With that, Issachar moved to the front of the flock and called them forward. Instantly, they obeyed. Joel wondered if sheep ever thought about living different lives, or if they were contented with the same routine day after day.

He cared for Laban and Dodo, but they were just dumb animals, after all. Maybe they felt happier with their lives than Joel did. He hoped so.

At home, he cleaned the dirt floor fouled by the sheep's droppings and put down fresh straw. Mother had the cook fire started, and Miriam had gone to the spring with a jug small enough for her to carry. Father was still upstairs, offering his morning prayers.

When Joel was finished his work, he climbed into the loft, took his place next to his father, and joined in the devotions. Then he gathered his scribe's tools—his brushes, the wooden pallet for his ink, pieces of much-used papyrus on which he wrote and rewrote his letters. Sometimes Joel could see the strange shapes even when he closed his eyes. Sometimes he dreamed of them. The straight lines would seem to wriggle and curve before him, then join one another in a kind of wild dance.

But many long days of copying and re-copying his letters were now giving way to time devoted to learning how the letters *did* join to form words, words which stood for things you could see and touch. Jars of oil and sheaves of grain. Head of cattle and sheep and goats. Horses and birds. Precious metals like copper and ores like iron. Who had decided that this group of letters meant "man," or that group meant "chariot"? It was a mystery, one that at times he longed to solve, but at other times wanted to leave behind and follow Issachar and the sheep into the pasturelands surrounding Jerusalem.

After the family had eaten their meal of bread, stewed onions and garlic, olives, and dried dates, Joel went with his father up through the city, toward the mountain called Zion, where Solomon had his palace and YAH his temple. The morning was perfect: a sun warm and shining, but air still cool in the shaded places. On the high street, they met Joel's friend Benjamin and his father, Mattan. Mattan and Joel's father had grown up together and were as close as brothers. Like Father, Mattan was a scribe, so Benjamin was being trained in the same profession. The two fathers walked a few strides ahead of their sons, exchanging the latest news and gossip from the city and Solomon's court. That allowed Joel and Benjamin to have their own conversations. Today, he was full of great news, but he teased Joel first, making him guess what it could be. When Joel threatened to break all his reed pens, Benjamin told what he knew

Two

"My father says that a caravan from Egypt is expected today!"

This *was* excellent news, worth having to try and guess it. "How does he know?" Joel asked.

"The Egyptians sent two men ahead of them to spread the word."

"When will the others arrive?"

"Father said this evening. He'll let me go into the market to see them. Will your father let you?"

"Of course!" In truth, Joel didn't know what his father would or wouldn't allow him to do. He had no particular use for Egyptians, and Joel's grandfather, one of the most important priests of YAH in all of Israel, had not one good thing to say about them. Nor would he let anyone forget that it was the Egyptians who had enslaved their ancestors and made them do forced labor to build treasure cities for Pharaoh. If YAH had not sent Moses, the deliverer, to bring the people out of Egypt, they would all still be there, living out their miserable lives under the lash of Pharaoh's slave drivers. Joel had heard the story many, many times. Grandfather never tired of relating it, and so dramatically that you might almost think he himself had been with Moses back during those days when YAH performed so many mighty wonders against Egypt. Water turned to blood, frogs, hail, darkness, boils—and at the end, the death of the firstborn. That part always made Joel ache on the inside.

But the Egyptians who came through Jerusalem were friendly, not charioteers bent on recapturing anyone. Not only that, but King Solomon had married the daughter of Pharaoh, so Israel had to be an ally of Egypt. If any problem did come up, Solomon had a mighty army, so no one would dare cross him.

Near their school, Joel and Benjamin passed the Tomb of King David, Solomon's father. They bowed their heads in respect to the great man who was not only a mighty warrior but also a poet and musician.

They entered the temple precinct through a side gate, and the boys said goodbye to their fathers, who continued to the Hall of Scribes, where they would compose and copy official documents. Some of these would be placed in the king's archives, and others would be sent to foreign nations, discussing matters of trade and diplomacy. Perhaps the wife of Solomon would speak a letter to her father, the Pharaoh, and a favored scribe would write down what she said. Then special messengers would dispatch it down the King's Highway. When Pharaoh received the letter, he could feel sure that his daughter's exact words were being read by his own scribes.

That was the work that lay ahead for Joel and Benjamin. First, though, they must perfect how to shape letters, then how to join them into words, then write them on sheets of papyrus. They were also being taught how to take dictation and read it back to themselves and each other to be sure they'd made no mistakes. Joel was a quick student, but sometimes, he wondered if he could ever learn all the things his father knew.

Sometimes he wondered if he *wanted* to learn all those things.

School was a building with one large central room lighted by windows high in the walls. To the sides were smaller rooms for storing scribes' equipment and a library of scrolls. The room had a smooth stone floor, always cool to the touch, even on hot summer days. Forty students worked there, divided into three groups. Joel and Benjamin, like the other members of the youngest group, had to do the most chores and put up with the taunts of the older boys, who often made fun of their ignorance and how many mistakes they made.

This morning, they were tasked with sweeping the entire room and bringing out the mats. While they worked, the middle group brought out the wooden pallets, brushes, ink, and pieces of papyrus used in copying. The oldest boys, as usual, did nothing useful, but enjoyed complaining about how lazy and stupid the younger boys were.

Joel didn't like it, but things would be better in the second year, and when he was a third-year student, he could order the others around.

When the room was cleaned to the satisfaction of Elishama, the head teacher, the boys took their mats and placed them in their assigned spots. The oldest boys had the best places. In the mornings, they sat where the sun would shine through the eastern windows, and in the afternoons, they moved to where the sun spread its golden glow from the west. The other boys squabbled over the remaining places, with the youngest students always the losers who ended up working in shadows all day long.

Joel and Benjamin sat next to each other, and though forbidden to speak during the work sessions, they had learned to communicate through expressions and gestures, especially when Elishama, who was very old, would forget what he'd been talking about and repeat himself three or four times.

The morning's work began as it always did, with the youngest students copying letters over and over so that they were formed alike, formed perfectly. Joel took up an unused piece of reed, crushed one end, and shaped it until he had a brush to his liking. Then he had to make several more for the older boys. They loved to complain that these brushes were the creation of baboons, and they wondered out loud how any serious scribe could be expected to produce superior work with such inferior tools. Joel, at least, had a knack for making brushes, so his were seldom rejected. But this morning, nothing he did pleased anyone. Jaziz, the leader of the oldest group, inspected his brushes, found them worthless even before trying any of them, and dropped them in Joel's lap.

"Why don't you make your own, then?" Joel asked him. "Since you're so great at everything."

The moment he spoke, he knew he was in trouble. Elishama, who had been instructing another boy, recognized his voice and came hurrying over.

"Why did you speak?" the old man challenged.

"I—"

"Silence!"

Joel wondered how he could answer the master's question *without* speaking.

"His brushes are trash!" Jaziz accused. "He doesn't belong in our school if he can't do better than this." Jaziz grabbed an offending example and held it before Elishama. The teacher inspected it carefully.

"I see nothing wrong with it. Perhaps you are too particular."

Joel wanted to agree that Elishama was exactly right, but he dared not say another word.

The teacher returned the brush to Jaziz. "See how it works before you reject it. Perhaps I should give all the little boys another lesson in how to prepare a superior brush."

I'm not a little boy, Joel thought.

"They need lots of lessons!" Jaziz exclaimed.

And you need a smack to wipe that stupid expression off your face, Joel thought.

Elishema looked hard at Jaziz. "Or perhaps *you* would prefer to instruct your younger classmates so that they can produce brushes worthy of your exacting standards."

Please not that, Joel thought. *The days are tiresome enough without Jaziz lording it over us.*

Jaziz immediately put Joel's fear to rest. "Oh, no!" he told Elishema. "I have lots of my own work to do, and besides, I don't have your skill, Master. No one can make a better brush than you!"

Joel glanced at Benjamin, who rolled his eyes. Everyone knew how Jaziz loved flattering their teacher. They also knew that Elishema realized it. He was old—his long white hair and beard, wrinkled skin, and limping gait told the tale—but he was no one's fool. Sometimes he looked as though *he* would enjoy giving Jaziz a smack. If he ever decided to, Joel hoped he would be there to enjoy it.

"Perhaps you are right," Elishema told Jaziz. "Your skills at brush-making could use some improvement, too. When I have time to teach the younger boys, you will join us."

Joel had to smile. But Jaziz glanced his way and caught him. Somehow, Joel knew he would get his revenge. The day had only started, and it was bad already.

It got much worse.

Joel mixed his ink and prepared to do the first copying exercise. His wooden palette had two carved wells for ink, one for black and one for red. Because he was still a first-year student, Joel was permitted to use only black ink. The red was more precious, used for special words such as names and for calling the reader's attention to the most important parts of a document. Joel longed for the time he'd be allowed to mix and use red ink along with black. Black had gotten to be his least favorite color. He was simply tired of it.

He set down to work. Elishama walked around the room, often stopping by a student to inspect his efforts. The students had to stand when he came by—how could an old man be expected to squat or kneel? Elishama was very strict. He himself, despite his age, still wrote a perfect hand, all his letters the same size and shape, each curve perfect and graceful. That came from many years' practice.

After a break for the students to use the latrine and drink water, Elishama gave dictation to the older boys. His droning voice made it difficult for Joel to concentrate. In fact, it began to lull him toward sleep.

Joel felt his eyes closing. The letters on his page went blurry. He hadn't slept much last night, so his head was insisting that he sleep *now*. if only he could put down his tools, lie on his side, and have a nap. But that was impossible. The boys were expected to work until Elishama gave them permission to stop.

Joel fought to concentrate, but it was no use. Then he heard the cries of birds outside, on their flight north. The others heard it, too. Many boys looked up, as if they could somehow see through the roof and watch the winged travelers.

"Keep to your work!" Elishama ordered. "The birds have their duty, and you have yours."

Then I wish I were a bird, Joel thought. Suddenly, the sheet of papyrus before him seemed hateful. So did the page from which he was copying. But he had to keep going.

Trouble lay ahead. First, Joel got too much ink on his brush and made a big splotch on his work sheet. He wiped it with a piece of cloth dipped in water, but a stain remained. He went back to his task, but now the letters began dancing in front on his eyes, the way they sometimes did in his dreams.

Then Joel found himself looking at one of the letters in particular. It was nothing more than some lines touching one another, but they were arranged to suggest an ox's head. Why hadn't he noticed that before? Before he knew what he was doing, Joel found himself adding lines for horns, then a mouth, ears, and a dot for an eye. He looked at his creation and felt satisfied. Another letter suddenly resembled a little house, so Joel added lines to make a door and a window. Another suggested a tiny man, so Joel added arms and drew a circle at the top for a head. A couple more touches with his brush, and the head had eyes, a nose, and a mouth. Then, without using any letter at all, Joel drew a flying bird. Then a bird with stick legs standing under a palm tree. Before he knew it, Joel had covered his piece of papyrus with drawings.

Then, Joel sensed someone was standing over him. He looked up, right into the stern face of Elishama. This was not good. Not good at all.

Three

"What in the name of YAH you are doing?" Elishama demanded.

Joel hung his head.

"Stand up!"

Joel obeyed.

"Show me!"

The room was silent. Joel felt all eyes on him. He wished he were a bird that could fly through one of the open windows.

"This, sir." Joel offered the sheet of papyrus to his teacher.

"Did I ask you to speak?" Elishama exclaimed.

Joel kept his eyes on the floor.

"So," Elishama declared after a careful study of Joel's work. "We have an *artist* in our midst! Like an Egyptian, this fellow likes to draw . . . " he paused to emphasize his point, "*pictures*! A house. A tree. An ox. And what's this? A . . . man!" He held the papyrus with his fingertips as though it were something unclean. Then he addressed the room: "Scribes do not make pictures of things. They make *words* that stand for things. Am I correct?"

All the boys instantly agreed. Who would dare go against Elishama when he was so outraged?

Elisahama brandished the papyrus in front of Joel's nose. "Who can tell me the penalty for foolishness like this?"

Across the room, Jaziz was quick to raise his hand. "A beating?" he suggested hopefully.

Other boys nodded and murmured agreement.

Joel kept his eyes fixed on the unyielding stone floor. "I meant no harm," Joel whispered.

"Were you asked to speak?" Elishama demanded.

"No, master. I am sorry."

"He is sorry," Elishama announced to the students. "And he should be, for he is old enough to know better."

Joel looked up and met Elishama's eyes.

"You *are* old enough to know better, are you not, Joel ben-Nathan?"

"Yes, master."

"And are your sorry for what you have done?"

"Yes."

"And do you agree that despite your sorrow, you must be punished?"

"I agree."

"Good! Since you have no taste for your assigned tasks today, we will find others for you." Elishama glanced around the room. All the students were looking at him expectantly. "Who here is thirsty?"

Every hand went up.

"Who needs a new brush?"

Every hand again.

"Your fellows have needs," Elishama informed Joel. "You will give them what they need."

So Joel spent the rest of the day serving his classmates. He brought water to every boy. All the oldest, at the suggestion of Jaziz, demanded several drinks, so Joel had to refill the jug again and again. Then he made new brushes. Then boys asked for fresh sheets of papyrus and to have their used pages scrubbed down and placed in the sun to dry. With their constant demands, Joel was kept scurrying from one task to another until the coming of late afternoon signaled the end of a torturous day.

Elishama told his students they need not roll up their mats or tidy the room; Joel would see that was done. They left, chatting and laughing. A few looked at Joel with sympathy, while Jaziz and the oldest boys shook their heads in contempt.

As they were being dismissed, Joel heard Elishama tell Benjamin to hurry to the Hall of Scribes and ask Joel's father to stop at the school before going home. Joel knew what that meant: his teacher himself would inform his father of his crime. When they got home, there would certainly be another punishment.

Before long, Father arrived. He listened in silence while Elishama informed him of Joel's misdeed and of its consequences. Father examined the offending sheet of papyrus and then surprised Joel by asking Elishama if he might have it.

"Your son must promise that he will never again break the rules of this school," Elishama warned. "If he does, he will not be allowed to return. Do you understand?" he asked, wagging his finger in Joel's face.

"Yes, master. I am sorry for what I did, and I will never do it again."

"Then you are forgiven. You may go."

Father thanked the old man, and they left. Joel expected that he would now receive a second lecture on his crime, followed by a just punishment when they got home. Joel had never been beaten, unlike Issachar and some of his other friends, whose fathers seldom spared the rod for bad behavior. He had seen the red welts on the back of Issachar's legs, and he could imagine how much they must hurt.

But Father said nothing, at least not at first. He kept inspecting the papyrus, turning it this way and that. The longer this went on, the more nervous Joel became. His father was most likely trying to come up with the worst punishment he could imagine.

When they were half-way home, Father spoke. "Tell me what happened today," he began. "This is not like you at all, son—to knowingly neglect your work and waste time with such scribblings."

"Last night, I couldn't sleep. The birds—they kept me awake."

"Which birds?"

"The ones that fly over Jerusalem. They call to each other all night long. They make me . . . " He was afraid to finish his thought.

"They make you what?" Father asked.

Joel shook his head. "I don't know."

"I see. You don't want to tell me, is that it?"

Joel said nothing.

Father touched his shoulder. "Very well. When you are ready, I hope you will. So what happened at school?"

"I was so sleepy, Father! I tried to do my work, but my eyes kept closing. Then the letters began moving around."

"Not really moving."

"No. It just seemed that way. Letters can't actually move on their own."

Father smiled. "Thank YAH for that! I will tell you a small secret: they do that to me sometimes, as well, when I'm tired or have a long text to copy. Other scribes admit the same thing."

That made Joel feel better.

"You wanted to sleep because you didn't sleep last night."

"Yes, sir."

"But Elishama wouldn't understand."

"No."

"He is strict."

"Yes."

"But why did you do *this*?" Father asked, holding the papyrus in front of them.

"I don't know! The letters started to—look like real things. I thought I would see if I could add anything to make them more real. Before I knew it, I had—drawn pictures."

"Which is not often done in Israel."

"I know."

"You've learned an important lesson today," Father told him. "I should add to Elishama's punishment. Do you agree?"

Joel could only nod.

"But I think you have suffered enough. Besides . . . "

Joel waited for what Father would say next. He looked at him and was surprised to see him smiling.

"Besides—you draw well. You have a keen eye for 'real things,' as you put it. If we were Egyptians, you would find much work among their painters, who are renowned for their art."

"But we're not Egyptians."

“No, but you *are* a scribe. A young one, but you have a gift. That may be why Elishama didn’t beat you or expel you from school.”

“Will you tell Mother?” Joel asked.

“Of course. After that, we need not speak of it any further. Do you agree?”

“Yes! Thank you, Father.”

Father tousled his son’s hair. “My secret Egyptian son! Now let’s hurry. Your mother will want our help, and I am very hungry.”

“Me, too,” Joel exclaimed.

The day had been bad enough, but not as terrible as he had feared.

Four

THEN things got much better. As they walked down the narrow street to their house, here came Miriam, running. Her face was beaming. "The Egyptians are here! The Egyptians are here! They're in the marketplace. Father, Mother says Joel and I can go with her to see what they have for sale. Is it all right? May we?"

Father laughed and pulled Miriam toward him. "What do you think, Joel?" he asked. "Do you want to go, or have you had enough of *Egyptian* things for one day?"

Joel had to smile at his father's joke. "Of course I do."

"Please, Father!" Miriam insisted. "Mother wants to look at what's for sale before it gets too dark."

"Then it's settled," Father said. "We'll all go!"

In truth, Joel couldn't imagine *not* seeing the caravan. All the neighbors would be there, and all his friends. Miriam grabbed Father's hand and tugged him forward. In a moment, they were at home, where Mother was waiting.

"I think we had better leave right now," Father said, "before this little one bursts with excitement." With Miriam leading the way, they made their way to the marketplace, joining a band of grownups and children, all talking excitedly.

The marketplace was crowded already. Torches blazed, making up for the waning light of the setting sun. Joel heard flutes, hand harps, and drums. Vendors cried their wares. Sheep coming in from the pastures bleated, and overhead, the birds continued calling.

Four

Joel's family moved toward the center of the open square, and there they were: Egyptians! You knew them right away by their strange dress. The men wore tunics of linen so light you could see their brawny chests and muscular arms through the fabric. At least they were all wearing loincloths underneath! No women had come with the traders, but the men wore collars of fancy beadwork in rainbow colors and shining metal armbands that looked like snakes entwined around their brown biceps.

Some of the Egyptians wore fancy wigs, with braids wrapped in bright cords and heavy with beads. Others had shaved their heads, and some had only one long hank of hair hanging down their backs. All the men's eyes were lined in black, and they smelled of spices, rubbed into their burnished skin with oils.

Joel had seen traders before, but these seem stranger than any travelers Jerusalem had ever welcomed.

"They put on a fine show," Father remarked.

"What do you mean?" Joel asked.

"Do you think that Egyptian men deck themselves in such outlandish costumes when they are at home, doing their daily work? For their heathenish festivals, perhaps, but not for ordinary days. They dress up like this because they know people will buy more from them if they look so exotic. In my opinion, it's indecent for men to show their bodies the way they do."

"Egypt is a burning hot land," Mother reminded him. "Perhaps the people there wear fewer clothes so that they can stand to live."

"It's hot here, too," Father noted. "But no Israelite man parades half-naked before a crowd of women and children."

Joel understood father's point. He glanced around the crowd and realized that all the Israelite men were dressed very much the same: a tunic to the knees, a light robe over that, and simple sandals. The women wore tunics to their ankles, robes over those, and head scarves, as well. He wondered if Egyptian men all dressed the way the traders did, what did their women wear? He felt somehow that it was better not to think about such a thing.

"Come, Mother!" Miriam urged. "Look!" She pulled Mother to a place where a trader had spread out a brightly patterned rug and was displaying necklaces and bracelets.

"I'm being summoned," Mother told Father, laughing. "We will meet you here later. I want to buy some things for my spice box. Mine is nearly empty."

"Very well," Father agreed.

Just then, Benjamin appeared. He whispered to Joel, "I was thinking your father would never let you come. Did he beat you?"

Joel looked to see if Father was listening, but Father had met two of his fellow scribes and they had their heads together, deep in talk. Joel wondered if Elishama had spread the news of his scandalous behavior. "No," Joel whispered back. "He talked to me and made me promise not to do anything like that again."

"That's all?" Benjamin looked almost disappointed.

"Well, not all. Father told me that I draw well." That boast felt good.

"He did?" Now Benjamin looked amazed.

"Father realizes I didn't mean any harm. I don't know what I was thinking."

"You can't use such an excuse again," Benjamin warned. "Next time, your father *will* beat you, and so will Elishama."

"I *won't* do it again," Joel vowed. "I've learned my lesson."

"The hard way," Benjamin added.

Just then, Father came to them. "Good evening, Benjamin," he said.

"Good evening, sir."

"Joel, we're going to see if the traders have papyrus for sale. Do you want to come with us, or would you rather spy out the land with Benjamin?"

This question was easily answered. Who wouldn't prefer time with a friend to having to tag along behind grownups and listen to their dull talk?

"I'll go with Benjamin."

Father nodded, as if he expected that answer. "Meet us back here later. And don't get into any trouble! You've had enough for one day."

Father raised his left eyebrow the way he did when he wanted to look especially serious.

"I'll behave," Joel promised. The men walked into the crowd.

"What now?" Benjamin asked.

"Come on," Joel suggested. "It's our big chance."

They made their way through the market, determined not to miss one thing. Right away, they came to a conjuror dressed in a purple robe embroidered with silver constellations. While the crowd watched, he pulled a dove from his sleeve and let it fly around the open marketplace. When he whistled, it returned to his hand. Then he brought forth a vial of some liquid, took a deep drink of it, grabbed a lighted torch, tilted his head back, brought the torch to his open mouth, and breathed out fire! The spectators oohed and aahed, and the people clapped. Then the man summoned a boy from the crowd and from behind his ear produced a small ball that gleamed like bronze.

"Sorcery," Benjamin declared. "Let's get away before he does something to us."

"Sorcery is just trickery," Joel replied. "Listen!"

He led the way to where some Egyptians were seated in a circle. Two played flutes, another plucked the strings of a hand harp, and the fourth beat a drum. In the middle of their circle, two boys, younger than Joel and Benjamin, performed a dance. It began slowly, with stately movements, but as the drumbeat got faster and the flutes and harp played louder, the dance became quicker, until the boys were whirling madly. The drummer urged them on with wild cries.

Joel couldn't help but tap his foot. He wanted to clap, to keep up with the beating of the drum. Then the music stopped without warning, and the dancers dropped to the dust. The crowd applauded, and the boys made their way around the circle, holding out their hands for money.

"Sorry," Joel told the smaller boy. "We have nothing to give you."

On they went, inspecting the traders' wares and trying not to stare at the men themselves. They came upon a man with a trained monkey. The little thing chattered and climbed over his shoulders and clung to his bald head. It even put a paw over one of his eyes. Every time the man would swat it away, the monkey would put it back. This had the children laughing and clapping.

Nearby sat a man cross-legged on a pillow, a large basket before him. He had a reed flute, from which he coaxed a slow, wandering tune that made no sense to Joel's ears. A younger man removed the lid from the basket and shook it. The weird music continued. Then, slowly, sinuously, the head of a serpent appeared over the lip of the basket. People gasped, and mothers pulled their little ones back to safety.

Still the music continued, and the flute player began to sway back and forth. More of the snake emerged out of the basket, and the creature reared up and spread its hood. A cobra!—the most deadly and feared serpent in all of Israel. It, too, began to sway, as if in time to the music. Back and forth it moved, its tongue flickering in and out.

The music continued and the man spoke to the serpent in the strange tongue of the Egyptians. Then, quickly, his assistant approached the basket and the snake slowly sank back inside it. The lid was firmly secured, and the performance was over.

Just then, Issachar appeared out of the crowd. He'd arrived at the market and was eager to see everything, but Joel didn't feel like doing things twice. Benjamin said he didn't mind taking Issachar around; besides, he wanted to see the conjuror again. The boys parted ways, and Joel wandered through the marketplace on his own.

The traders were offering pottery, dried fruits, sheer fabrics as light as air, many spices in small wooden boxes, and fine papyrus scrolls. There were tiny clay figurines of all kinds of animals. Joel identified horses, camels, foxes, lions, and bears, but others, like a creature with a bumpy back, a narrow snout with bared teeth, and a long tail, he did not recognize. He had no money, but it didn't matter. Nothing he saw called out for him to buy it.

But he could still hear the music, and he found himself making his way back to where the boys danced to the flute, harp, and drum.

The dance was again in progress, faster and faster, and wilder than before. When it was done, the crowd cheered appreciation, and the two boys stood and nodded their heads, accepting the praise. Then people went on their way, looking for other entertainment. The musicians and the bigger boy went into a tent pitched nearby. Joel did not move. Then the smaller of the two dancers noticed him and held up a finger, as if to tell Joel to wait a moment. He disappeared into the tent and came back carrying a sturdy sack. Something inside it was moving vigorously, as if trying to escape. What was it? Not a cobra, certainly! Still, Joel took a step back. The boy sat on the mat where the drummer had been and gestured to Joel to sit beside him.

I could get into trouble, Joel thought. *I shouldn't do this.*

But he did.

Five

Joel looked at the other boy. His feet were bare, and he wore only a loincloth and a single strand of colored beads. Like the other Egyptians, his eyes were circled in black, as if he had used a brush and writing ink to paint around them. He was bald except for a single long braid growing from the side of his head. Like the other Egyptians, he smelled not of sweat, even though he was dripping with it from the exertion of his dance, but rather of spices. His arms and legs were as thin as the legs of the cranes that flew over Jerusalem, as if he seldom received enough to eat. How many years did he have? Certainly, fewer than Joel did, perhaps nine. Joel could only guess.

The Egyptian held the bundle in his lap, and whatever was inside kept pushing against the cloth. It strained to escape its confinement.

The other boy gestured to Joel, informing him he was about to open the bundle, and asking if Joel was willing for that to happen. Joel nodded. He held his breath while the sack was untied, and out of the opening appeared the head of—

A cat.

A bronze-colored cat with alert golden eyes, long white whiskers, pointed ears, and a strange ebony marking on its forehead that looked something like a beetle.

Joel somehow knew it was a cat, even though he had never seen one alive before that moment. There were no cats in Jerusalem. Dogs, yes, for they were useful in helping herd sheep and for alerting their masters of dangerous animals like lions. Some of Joel's neighbors kept dogs, but Father would not allow any in his house. He said that having to deal with two sheep was quite enough.

The cat looked all around, climbed out of the sack, but made no effort to leave the grasp of the boy, who kept whispering to it in a low voice.

Joel could not take his eyes away from the creature, and when the cat peered back at him, he felt a shiver run down his back. Never had he looked into the eyes of any animal that seemed so—so *knowing*. You could stare into Laban and Dodo's eyes all day long and never discover the slightest sign of intelligence. They were as dumb as the dust beneath their feet. But *this* one . . .

The animal blinked, licked a paw, and then the boy released his hold. The cat stretched and stepped carefully onto the ground in front of Joel, who scooted back. Would the creature bite him? Scratch his leg? Or put a spell on him with its large, golden eyes?

"Ta-Muit," said the Egyptian, pointing to the animal that was now rubbing its face against his bare brown leg. "Ta-Muit."

Joel spoke no Egyptian, and he suspected that the other boy spoke no Hebrew. "Ta-Muit," the other boy repeated, pointing to the cat, whose nonchalance made Joel want to laugh. Then the other boy pointed to himself: "Seb."

"It's your name?" Joel asked.

The boy nodded. "Seb."

Joel pointed to himself: "Joel."

"Joel," repeated the Egyptian.

"Seb," Joel said, pointing to the boy. "Ta-Muit," he added. The cat, acknowledging its name, came to him. Now he had an even better look at it. It was not very large, so one could easily pick it up and hold it the way Seb had been doing. Its whole body was bronze but covered with deep brown spots. The hair beneath its chin was pure white, and a single black stripe ran from its head all the way down its back and on to the tip of its tail.

Seb stroked the cat's side. The cat began making a strange noise, not a growl, but a low, soft sound something like Joel's father's snoring. The Egyptian pointed to Joel's hand and then to the cat. Joel understood.

Should he touch it? What would his father say? Then he wondered why he needed permission to pet Ta-Muit. What could be the harm?

Joel touched the cat's back. Its fur was soft, even softer than Laban's or Dodo's wool. Ta-Muit bumped its head against Joel's hand. Seb smiled and gestured for Joel to scratch the cat's head. Joel did, and the cat made more of that same odd sound, coming from somewhere deep in its throat. The other boy nodded and smiled, as if to say, "See, the cat likes you."

Joel liked it, too.

Then one of the musicians came out from the tent, sat next to Seb, and grinned at Joel. "You enjoyed the dancing? I noticed you moving your feet. You wanted to join in, didn't you?" The man was speaking Hebrew!

Joel was surprised. "Excuse me, sir, but I didn't know you speak our language."

"Of course I do! And Akkadian, Hittite, and Hurrian. When you're a traveler like me, it's best to understand what people are saying to—and about—you. Do you know any languages besides Hebrew?"

"No, sir. But I am learning how to write and to read."

"Ah, smart fellow," the Egyptian declared. "Good for you. I can speak six languages but can't write my own name in any of them."

Meanwhile, the cat, Ta-Muit, kept moving between the man, Seb, and Joel, looking for someone to pet it.

"You admire our cat?" the man asked Joel.

"Yes, sir."

"Would you like to buy it? It's for sale. Very good for catching and killing mice and rats. The price is cheap. It would be a good investment."

The moment the man announced that Ta-Muit was for sale, Seb pulled the cat close to his chest and shook his head. *He must know some Hebrew,* Joel thought.

Seb spoke to the man, pleading for something.

The man raised his hand to Seb, who ducked his head and held up an arm across his face. The man merely smiled, but his eyes were hard.

"The boy is attached to the animal," he explained. "In a moment of weakness, I allowed him to bring it with us from Memphis. What a mistake! It's been nothing but trouble ever since. I have been tempted to do away with it more than once, but it would upset the boy."

Joel was horrified to think that the Egyptian would kill the cat, who looked at him impassively.

Seb, on the other hand, had lowered his head and kept the animal close. The man said something, and the boy seemed relieved.

"I told him not to worry. I will not harm the creature, but I *will* sell it, if I can get my price."

Seb shook his head and looked at the man imploringly.

The man chuckled. "See what I must put up with? It makes me weary."

"Is he your son?" Joel asked.

The man glanced at Seb and scoffed. "By Amun, no! He is an orphan. His parents went boating on the Nile and were attacked by a hippopotamus. It killed them both, and the lad had no one else. I found him starving in the streets and took him in. To repay me, he dances."

Poor Seb! Joel thought. It was terrible to think of losing your parents, and of having no family to look after you. From the way Seb had acted to defend himself, Joel suspected that there were times when the man beat him.

He had a question. "What, sir, is a hippotapitus?"

"A hippopotamus, you mean?"

"Yes, sir."

"You don't know?"

"No, sir."

"It's a mighty beast that rules the Nile, along with the terrifying crocodile. The hippopotamus lurks beneath the water and attacks those who dare swim or launch boats nears its home. Its mouth is so large it could swallow a boy like you in one gulp. And its teeth! As thick as your arm, and as sharp as a battle lance. None can capture it. None can tame it. Even the gods fear it."

Was such a thing possible? Joel found it hard to believe, but he hoped it was true. The largest creature of the water he had ever seen was a fish two cubits long. He could scarcely imagine a monster whose mouth could swallow him whole. No, the man had to be telling him a tale.

"You don't believe me?" The man seemed able to read his thoughts. "They rightly say that you Israelites know nothing about the world outside your borders. For you, it's shabby cities on the tops of rocky hillocks and villages of peasants trying to scrape a living from the desert."

Joel felt insulted. Should he say something? Yes, he had to. "Jerusalem is a great city. Our king has untold wealth. Have you seen his palace? And the temple of YAH that stands on top of Mount Zion?"

"Yes, I have. They are well enough, in their way. But have *you* seen the pyramids, or the avenue of sphinxes between Karnak and Luxor?"

"What is a sphinx?"

The man laughed. "See? You make my point for me! You don't know the hippopotamus or the temples and pyramids of my country."

In the man's eyes, Joel must have seemed as ignorant as Laban and Dodo did to him. At that moment, he envied Seb, who had perhaps seen these wonders for himself—a fair trade, perhaps, for not having a mother or father. But no, that could not be right. A family was the most important thing in the world—after being one of YAH's own people.

"You've never seen a living cat before, have you?" the trader asked.

Joel admitted he had not.

"As I said, this one is yours, if you can pay."

Joel felt that if he had all the gold he could carry, he would not buy Ta-Muit and take the creature away from Seb.

“I am sorry,” Joel told him. “I have no money.”

“Which is exactly what all you fine citizens of Jerusalem say! ‘We have no money.’ How is that possible when the wealth of your King Solomon is legendary? I do not understand the people of this city.”

“What are you doing?” asked a serious voice behind him. Startled, Joel jumped to his feet. He knew it was Father, and he knew that Father was not pleased.

Six

"Just looking at this cat, Father. I've never seen one before."

"And I hope you never will see another after these—*strangers* leave Jerusalem. Cats are an abomination. The Egyptians worship them!" He glared at the man. Then he said something to the man Joel didn't understand. He recognized it as Egyptian. Another surprise: Joel had no idea his father spoke that language.

"You speak Egyptian well," the trader replied in Hebrew.

"I am a scribe," Father answered. "It helps in my work."

"This boy—your son— I suppose, liked our music and dancing, and my helper was simply being friendly."

"Your slave, you mean," Father replied severely.

"Ah, no, my friend. He is an orphan and is like an adopted son to me."

"So you say." Father addressed Joel. "Come along. It's time to meet your mother and sister."

Joel wanted to protest that he'd done nothing wrong, but his father seemed in no mood to argue. He glanced at Seb, who was keeping the cat close to his chest. If he felt anything, it was hidden behind an expression like a mask.

"I offered to sell the cat to your son," the trader told Father. "A fair price. Your boy likes the animal, and it will keep away the rats from your home."

"Who says there are rats in my house?" Father demanded.

The Egyptian shrugged. "Are there not rats everywhere, my friend?"

"I am not your friend. Keep your cat, for we're not interested." Then Father looked at Seb and his face softened. "May YAH protect and keep you, lad."

Seb seemed to understand Father's tone, if not the words. He nodded, eased Ta-Muit back into the sack, and went to the tent. Before he entered, he gave Joel a sorrowful look. Then he was gone.

"It goes ill with men who beat children without cause," Father told the Egyptian. "Look to yourself, for YAH is watching you."

"YAH is not the god of Egypt," the man countered. "What would he care for the likes of me?"

"He sees and judges those who are within the borders of Israel," Father shot back.

"Then I had best be on my way."

"As quickly as possible," Father agreed.

"Good night, my friend," the man replied. He snatched up his mat and made his way into the tent without a backward glance.

"Are you cross with me?" Joel asked.

"No. I sometimes wonder why you do what you do, but that's not unusual for fathers. When I was about your age, your grandfather often said he could not understand most of what I did. We had many—what shall I call them?—*disagreements*."

Joel could believe that, for his grandfather thought he was right about any matter he cared to discuss.

"You liked the music?" Father asked.

"Yes, sir. Was that wrong?"

"No. You've heard much music in the temple, in praise of YAH. But music can be used for other things, as well, not all of them holy."

Charming the cobra was like that. What could be holy about a snake?

"We should find your mother and your sister," Father said. As they moved through the crowd, he spoke again about the Egyptian boy. "What did the man tell you about him?"

"That he was an orphan, and his parents were killed by a giant creature that lives in the Nile River. I can't remember its name."

"A tall tale," Father declared. "The poor child is slave to that scoundrel. He looks half-starved, and one can only imagine how often he's beaten."

No wonder Ta-Muit is so precious to him, thought Joel. *Perhaps he has no other friends.*

"Did you see anything you would like to have?" Father asked.

"No, sir."

"I found these." Father held up a sheaf of papyrus. "Excellent quality, and a good price. These pesty traders are good for something, after all."

In a few moments, they spied Mother and Miriam. Mother had found the spices she wanted, and Miriam was wearing the new necklace and bracelet Mother had helped her choose.

"But what about you?" Mother asked Joel. "You found nothing?"

"I found a cat!" Joel blurted.

"A cat?" Miriam cried. "A real, live one? Oh, where is it? I want to see it. Can I, Father? Mother? Please?"

"No, indeed," Father declared. "It's gone, anyway."

"What did it look like?" Miriam asked Joel. "Tell me!"

"Not now," Father said. "You may ask him later, when I don't have to hear about it."

"I listened to music and saw two boys dancing," Joel went on. "I—liked it."

"Egypt," Father sighed. "Always a temptation."

"Let's go home," Mother told Miriam. "Nathan, stay with Joel and see if there isn't something he would like. It doesn't seem fair that only he gets nothing. After all, it's not often that the traders come to Jerusalem."

"For which I'm glad!" Father exclaimed. But then he beamed at Miriam. "Still, Little Star looks beautiful with her new jewelry. And I look forward to one of your delicious stews," he told Mother. "Seasoned with the spices of Egypt!"

"Help him find something," Mother urged. "We'll see you at home."

Six

Father and Joel strolled through the market again. Some people had already done their buying and gone, but many people remained.

"Is there anything you would like?" Father asked.

Ta-Muit, Joel thought. The idea was so impossible that it made him smile at his own foolishness. He found nothing he wanted, and Father declared there was no reason to waste one's money on things he did not need. Joel returned home empty-handed.

Since they had stayed at the market so long, it was soon time for sleep. Mother warmed some stew and they ate a quick meal. Tomorrow, she promised a special dish, prepared with the spices she had purchased. Miriam insisted on wearing her new necklace and bracelet to bed, and Father remarked how he looked forward to trying a new sheet of papyrus.

They soothed Laban and Dodo so that they would sleep, and then all climbed to the loft room.

Father prayed the night blessing over the family, and soon all was quiet.

Everyone slept. Everyone except Joel, that is. He lay in the darkness, just as he had the night before, listening to sounds: his father's snoring, the cries of a nighthawk, the faint murmur of men talking somewhere outside. Here was his life. He had food for his belly and clothing for his body. He was being trained for a fine career as a scribe, and because his father was highly skilled and worked in the king's court, they had enough of what they needed, even a little extra for nice things like his sister's new jewelry. He should be satisfied with the life YAH had decreed for him.

But he wasn't. How ungrateful he was! He kept thinking about Seb, whose parents had been killed by the monster of the Nile. Was Seb sleeping now, or still being made to perform in the marketplace? And would his master beat him this night?

Perhaps it was well with Seb. Perhaps his master had been pleased with him and had given him plenty to eat, a warm covering, and permission to sleep in the open air. Would he be safe from snakes and scorpions, or rats that some of the old women claimed would nibble off the toes of children who did not obey their parents? Joel knew that his life was better than Seb's, but Seb had things that Joel did not: the chance to see wondrous new things. The great pyramids at Giza, the avenue of sphinxes, perhaps even the monstrous creatures lurking in the Nile. Maybe he had been to the great sea that lay to the west of Israel, a sea so big you could sail in it forever and never come to its far shore.

One thing Seb had for certain that made Joel envy him:

His cat.

Wherever Seb was sleeping this night, be it in the tent his master had pitched or under the sky, Joel felt certain that Ta-Muit was nearby.

What was it like to own a cat? Joel himself owned few things—his clothes, his reed brushes. The idea of having his own animal—that was impossible. Yes, the family had Laban and Dodo, but they belonged to his father, and they were kept only because of what they could provide: wool for spinning and weaving, milk for making cheese, and—one day when they were old—food for the table. Some of Joel's neighbors had dogs, but only to help herd and protect their flocks. There were some stray dogs in the city, roaming freely and picking up scraps where they could. King Solomon was known to keep many animals; you could hear them sometimes as you passed along the walls of his palace. There were monkeys and rare birds with spreading tails and breasts bluer than the evening sky. Once in a while, you could hear wild roaring from the palace, for the King kept forty lions to guard his throne, or so it was said. Father laughed at that idea, and he remarked that some people had a bad habit of greatly exaggerating the truth. He did know for a fact, however, that the king had two cheetahs, for his fellow scribe, Ishhod, had seen them with his own eyes. Ishhod told Father they resembled lions but were covered all over with spots, had long tails, and lacked the thick mane of hair for which male lions were famous. YAH had blessed them with sleek bodies and long, long legs made for bursts of incredible speed when they hunted. Ishhod had also told Father that the king did not keep cheetahs because he wished to use them in the hunt. No, he kept them because their beauty pleased him. They were, Ishhod had remarked with disapproval, the king's "pets."

"Pets." That was a strange word, and a strange idea. Why keep an animal just because it pleased you? Animals were created by YAH for people's use—sheep for milk and cheese and wool. Goats for milk and hides. Chickens for eggs and meat. Oxen to pull the plow. Bees for honey. Donkeys to ride upon. Even the hawks and falcons used by members of Solomon's court had their purpose, to hunt pigeons and doves for the king's table.

But only kings could afford to keep animals just because they were pleasing.

Joel drifted toward sleep. He thought of Ta-Muit, and he realized that he wanted a cat like that, a cat just because its presence was pleasing. A cat to be—his pet.

Seven

“Miriam, stop pushing on me.” Joel whispered the words, afraid to wake his family. But his sister kept bumping into his leg, as she sometimes did when she was dreaming.

“Stop,” he said again, reaching for the blanket and turning on his side, away from Miriam. Then he felt it. Something was nuzzling his foot. A hungry rat sent to nibble off his toes because he’d been disobedient in school yesterday! Joel shook his leg to scare it away. He sat up and peered around to see if the intruder was gone.

His eyes were used to the darkness, and they were helped by a silver moonlight shining through the window. He could discern something, but it wasn’t a rat—not a living one, anyone. No, it was —

Ta-Muit with a dead rat in its jaws!

I’m dreaming, Joel thought. *Ta-Muit is with Seb.*

Joel looked again. The cat was still there. It looked back at him, then dropped its prize onto the mat.

“What are you doing here?” Joel whispered. He looked to where Miriam was sleeping. Across the room came the sounds of his father’s snoring, his mother’s quiet breathing.

Ta-Muit was no dream. He rubbed against Joel’s calf as if he wanted to be thanked for the verminous gift. Then he started to make that strange noise again.

“Be quiet!” Joel hissed. “Do you want to wake everybody?” He sounded just like his mother, scolding Father.

Joel got to his knees and reached for the cat. Would it bite him? That didn't seem likely, but he wasn't sure. After all, he'd never seen a cat in his life until this evening, let alone touch one. But Ta-Muit was acting friendly, and when Joel took the animal into his arms, it rubbed the top of its head against his chest.

He had to get the cat out of the house. What would his father and mother say if they knew it was there?

As quietly as he could, Joel started down the ladder. Ta-Muit had stopped making that strange sound, so perhaps Joel had the chance of getting him gone without being detected.

"Joel, what are you doing?"

It was his father.

"I'm thirsty. I'm going down to get a drink."

"All right. But be quiet."

"I will."

He hadn't been found out!

Once downstairs, Joel started for the door. He hoped that Laban and Dodo would not rouse. If they did, they would wake the whole house.

Joel realized that he *was* thirsty, so he put Ta-Muit down and got himself a dipper of water. The cat made a noise that sounded like "mau," stood up on its hind legs, and pawed at Joel's knee.

"You're thirsty, too?" Joel whispered.

Ta-Muit kept making his "mau" sound, and Joel refilled the dipper and held it down on the packed earth floor. The cat instantly began lapping from it and drank until it was empty.

Joel couldn't help but smile when he thought what his mother would say—or do—if she found out that a *cat* had been drinking from the dipper they all used.

"You have to go," Joel told the cat. He pushed open the door and stepped into the street. "Come on," he said. "Out here."

Ta-Muit obeyed. Joel listened. No sounds anywhere. No baby cried, no dog barked. Above him, the stars gleamed like silver beads. Dawn was a long time away, and Jerusalem slept.

Joel squatted and petted the cat. "How did you get into the house?" he asked. "The door was closed."

But not the window in the upstairs room, Joel realized. Somehow, Ta-Muit had climbed high enough to come in.

"Why aren't you with Seb?" Joel asked, even though he knew the cat could not answer. He opened the door and pushed it into the street. "I wish you could stay, but you can't. You have to go back."

Ta-Muit simply looked at him.

"Go on! And thanks for the rat—I think."

Still, the cat did not move. Joel made himself shut the door. It was hard to do it, because everything in him wanted to bring Ta-Muit back into the house, wake his family, and tell them that YAH had brought him the pet he had prayed for, without even realizing that he *had* prayed.

All was still.

Then Joel realized there was a dead rat upstairs. He had to get rid of it or find a way to explain it in the morning. Up he climbed. Joel found the creature at the bottom of his mat. He didn't want to touch it, for it was foul, unclean. But he had no choice. He took it by the tail and dropped it out the window.

Then Joel lay down again, pulled some cover away from Miriam, and tried to get comfortable. He stared into the darkness and felt sorry for himself.

EIGHT

BIRD cries awakened him. Joel wondered for a second if Ta-Muit's nocturnal visit had been only a dream. It was still dark, with only the faint light before sunrise entering the room. He wanted to sleep more, but there was something he had to find out. Joel pushed back his cover and sat up. He stretched and yawned as loudly as he could.

"Joel?" his mother asked.

"Yes, Mama. I'm going to get up. I have to use the latrine."

"Go on, then. We'll all be up soon."

He climbed down the ladder, pulled on sandals, and opened the door. *Please let Ta-Muit be here,* he prayed. Right away he wondered if that was a proper thing to ask YAH. It must not have been, for the street was empty. Instead of heading to the latrine that several families shared, Joel hurried toward the market. He had to see Seb, find out if Ta-Muit had escaped, and if he had, how he'd managed to find Joel's house and a way through a second-story window.

He was running, but there was no one to ask him where he was going in such a hurry. In a short time, he bounded into the market square, expecting to find the tents and displays of goods all still in place. Surely the traders would have some fires lit, both for cooking and for warmth, since the morning was cool.

But the square was empty. The caravan had left! But why go in such a hurry? And who had opened the city gate for them?

All Joel found were pieces of litter—bits of rope, ashes from fires, the rinds of melons, the brown papery skins of onions, scraps of cloth, a scattering of bright beads from where a necklace had broken.

Joel scanned the square. Maybe, just maybe, Ta-Muit was lurking somewhere nearby. But would he want to leave Seb, who loved him so well? Perhaps Seb's master had sold him last night, and the cat had escaped from a strange new owner. If so, why?

Because he wanted to be with me, Joel decided.

A foolish idea. More likely, Ta-Muit had gone back to Seb after bringing Joel its farewell gift. Certainly the cat was with the caravan and with Seb, its rightful owner. They were on the road to the north, each step taking them farther away from Jerusalem.

From himself.

For a second, Joel thought of running to the city gate to see if he could catch up with them, find out if Ta-Muit was there, and if so, at least say goodbye.

But he couldn't do that. He was expected at home, and he didn't feel like explaining why he'd gone to the marketplace. There was nothing for it except to return and act as if nothing unusual had happened during the night.

And that's what Joel did.

While they were eating the morning meal, Issachar came by to get Laban and Dodo. He had exciting news: "Mother agreed that I can stay in the field with my brother tonight! We'll keep your sheep and the others with us, too, if that's all right."

"That's good news, Issachar," Father said. "You're growing up and getting more responsibilities."

"Yes, sir. I wish . . . "

Joel knew what Issachar was going to say.

"Yes?" Father asked.

"That Joel could come with me this morning and stay overnight with us in the fields."

"May I?" Joel said.

Father shook his head. "You both know that's impossible. Joel, you have your own responsibilities. After what you did at school yesterday, you can't miss today."

"What happened yesterday?" Issachar asked.

"I'll tell you later," Joel put in. "It's nothing all that important." He could feel Father's eyes on him, and he wondered about the sin of lying.

"Then can he come after school?"

"Not today," Father said.

So the matter was settled. There was no point in arguing. But then Father offered hope. "Perhaps some other night. Sometime soon. You'd like that, Joel?"

"Oh, yes, sir!"

"Very well. Sometime soon."

Suddenly, the day seemed brighter.

"I have to get going," Issachar said. "Father scolds me if I'm late."

The sheep, untied, made for the door just as they always did.

"Behave yourselves today," Father warned them. "Don't give Issachar reason to beat you."

"Nathan!" exclaimed Mother. "He doesn't beat the sheep. Do you, Issachar?"

"No, ma'am. We're gentle with them. Besides, these two are always obedient."

"Just like this one here," Father joked.

"Father!" Joel protested. "I'm obedient."

Father's left eyebrow went up. "Most of the time."

"I have to go," Issachar said. "See you tomorrow evening."

Then it was time to end the meal so that Joel could get to school. It would not do to be late.

He arrived on time, and the first thing he had to face was the smirking face of Jaziz. "Here's the picture-drawer," he remarked to a couple of the other students. "What are you going to draw for us today, little Egyptian?"

Joel ignored him. He gathered his mat and tools and settled into his usual place near Benjamin.

"You really didn't get a beating last night?" was the first thing Benjamin wanted to know.

"I told you, no!" Joel said, annoyed. He was bursting to tell Benjamin all about Ta-Muit and the great adventures of the past night, but there was no time now. Elishama appeared, commanded his students to find their places and get prepared to work.

When they were settled, Elishama led the class through morning prayers. As the old man intoned them, Joel felt his mind drifting away toward other things—conjurors, snake charmers, and Egyptian cats. *Stop!* he ordered himself. *YAH is not pleased with people who only pretend to pray.* He had heard that warning from his grandfather many times.

When prayers were over, Elishama addressed the class. "You all know what happened with Joel ben-Nathan yesterday."

Joel felt that every eye was on him. He kept his eyes straight ahead, looking at his teacher.

"He has been disciplined," Elishama went on. "I am certain that all of you are grateful for his faithful service to you, and that you find his brushes more than satisfactory." Here he looked directly at Jaziz. "Joel has done his penance and has promised that he will never again neglect his studies or indulge in pagan scribblings. His fault has been discovered, repented, and punished. That is the end of it! Any boy found taunting him, or even calling to his attention what he did yesterday, will be disciplined. Do you understand?"

The others promised that they did. "Very well, then," Elishama said. "Now get on with your studies."

Everyone did. Joel felt grateful for Elishama's warning, but he was smart enough to suspect that Jaziz and the others would find ways to torment him when their teacher was not nearby. Joel had a hard time keeping his mind on his work. Twice he wrote a wrong letter, and three times he took too much ink into his brush and messed the papyrus. He quickly washed the place so that no one could tell he'd made mistakes. If Elishama stopped more often than usual to inspect Joel's work, perhaps that was to be expected.

Eight

All Joel could think about were Seb and Ta-Muit. He kept wishing he had an animal like that for his own, something so beautiful and friendly. He felt sure the cat liked him. Hadn't it rubbed against his legs and allowed him to scratch behind its ears? Hadn't it made its way through the maze of streets from the market to his house? Hadn't it discovered a way to the loft where Joel and his family slept? And hadn't Ta-Muit presented Joel the gift of a dead rat?

When he wasn't thinking about Ta-Muit, Joel had his mind on the Egyptians and their caravan. On Seb and his journey to the north. What would he see? Lions and bears in the wilderness? Oases with palm trees and pools of clear water? Was the road dangerous? Joel had heard that it was the home of robbers and murderers lying in wait for unwary travelers. Could the Egyptians defend themselves? An attack against the caravan sounded frightening, but also exciting. Joel imagined himself brandishing a sword, slicing off the head of a hideous bandit and saving Seb from being taken prisoner. It would be dangerous, for sure, but worth it.

Nine

Compared to the life of a warrior, existence in Jerusalem was horribly plain, ordinary—like stew without salt. Why did some boys his age have to stay in one place, while others got to go on adventures? Even Issachar would have a night in the fields, where the shepherds built fires and gathered to trade stories.

The day dragged on. No one bothered him. That, at least, was a blessing.

Father came for Joel just when the students were being released. Benjamin and his father joined them on the way home. After they bid them goodbye, Father invited Joel to join him at the temple for the evening sacrifice. This was a privilege reserved for the older boys, and Father had never asked Joel before.

"You'd like to come with me?" Father wanted to know.

"Yes, sir. May I?"

"It's time. You'll soon be a man. You're old enough to worship as a man worships."

At home, Joel and Father washed and put on clean clothes. Mother promised her special stew once they returned from the temple. As the sun began to set, Joel and his father headed out to Mt. Zion, the crowning point of the city, where YAH had chosen to live in the temple he had appointed King Solomon to build.

They were joined by other men of all ages. Benjamin's father met them, but Benjamin was not with him. Joel figured that Benjamin's father didn't yet consider him old enough to take part in the men's worship. Joel felt proud to be walking next to his father and to see how the other men greeted him. At that moment, Joel wanted to grow up and be like his father—a scribe, blessed by YAH with the ability to read and write, a man respected in Jerusalem, which was, after all, the most important city in all Israel. In all the world.

Egyptian tradesmen, Egyptian tricks, Egyptian music and dance—all seemed far away. Seb, his adventures and his dangers, Ta-Muit—all parts of a dream that was not intended for Joel. No, his life was here in Jerusalem, and he felt satisfied.

But the very next moment, his thoughts and his longings were for the road north, and nights under the stars, and the avenue of sphinxes, and river monsters, and—Ta-Muit.

It didn't take long to climb to the top of Mt. Zion. They entered the outer court and Joel looked at the temple. He had known it since he was a child, but every time he saw the building, pride and what his father called "holy fear" rose in him.

The court was crowded with men and boys. Women stayed at home, according to the tradition. Joel stood as tall as he could to get the best view. Soon, the priests appeared in their robes.

"You don't have to watch this part if you don't want to," Father whispered.

"I want to," he whispered back. Father put a reassuring hand on his shoulder.

A lamb was brought forth. Its bleating was the only sound. A priest held it firmly while another quickly slit its throat. Blood poured out of the wound and the animal went limp.

Joel knew about such sacrifices. Everyone did. Daily offerings were part of temple services. But he'd never seen the cutting of the throat with his own eyes. He was sorry he had looked, but he was glad that he had. The priest smeared lamb's blood over the altar. A sigh swept over the crowd of men and boys, as if everyone had been holding his breath, and now all could be released.

A priest took fire from the bloody altar and carried it inside the temple, where Joel knew it would be used to light the incense on a second altar and consume offerings of grain and wine. Even outside in the courtyard, Joel could smell the incense. This part was not so bad, but he couldn't stop seeing the flash of the knife blade across the lamb's throat. Why did that have to be? Why did YAH command sacrifices of innocent lambs? The priests offered prayer and the singers chanted. Many in the crowd knew the words, and Joel joined in when he could.

When it was over and the crowd was walking down from the temple, Joel felt grown up. Some of Father's friends remarked that this was the first time they'd seen Joel at a temple service. One man assured Father that Joel was several fingers taller than just a month ago. Another asked if that was not the beginning of a man's beard on Joel's upper lip. He puffed out his chest and agreed that yes, he had grown. He was Joel ben-Nathan, scribe of Jerusalem, soon to take his place among the men of his city.

And then the image of Ta-Muit came bounding into his mind, and he knew that he yearned to be in some desert oasis, listening to Egyptian tales of the endless Nile and monsters with teeth as large as his arms and mouths big enough to swallow him whole.

What was happening to him? One minute he wanted one thing; the next second, his mind was changed. Maybe the Egyptians had put a spell on him.

It was all so confusing.

At home, Mother and Miriam had the meal waiting. The stew was delicious, and it contained enough salt. They ate bread with it, and mother surprised them with some dried dates she had bought from the Egyptians. They were sweeter than any that grew in Israel, Mother declared.

After the meal, they sat on wooden benches in front of the house. This was a good time for families and friends to visit one another, to tell stories of their people. Tonight, Father recounted tales of the great King David, and how when he was just a lad not much older than Joel, he had defended his flock from both lion and bear. Father knew how to tell a story well, and he could scare you one moment and make you laugh the next.

Soon it was time for bed. For once, Joel slept deeply. When he awoke the next morning, the sacrifice of the lamb was the first thing to come into his mind. He could hear its bleating, then its final gasp as the knife cut into its throat . . .

Joel opened the door to go outside and use the latrine. On the threshold were two dead rats and one dead mouse. And there, sitting patiently across the street, looking directly at him, was Ta-Muit. Joel's heart felt like singing.

"Ta-Muit!" he exclaimed. "What are you doing here?"

In answer, the animal came to him and rubbed its muzzle against his leg. Then it returned to where its victims lay sprawled in the dust. It sniffed, pawed at them, and then came back to Joel. Inside the house, he heard his family getting up.

"What am I going to do with you?" Joel said to the cat. "You can't stay." Ta-Muit just looked at him. "But I *want* you to stay!" Joel cried. "I want you to be my cat."

Just then Joel's father appeared in the doorway. "Who are you talking to?" he asked. Then he saw Ta-Muit. "What in the world?" he cried. "Is this the cat that was with the Egyptians?"

"Yes, sir."

"How can it be *here*, then? They left Jerusalem before dawn yesterday."

"I don't know," Joel said. "I opened the door—here it is." He decided not to tell his father about Ta-Muit's visit two nights before.

"It should have gone with the traders. Cats have no place in Israel, least of all here in Jerusalem, where YAH dwells. It cannot stay."

"Where will it go? The traders are far away by now. How can it find them?"

"Chase it away, and if it insists on trying to come back, I will deal with it."

Joel knew what that meant. "No!" he exclaimed. "Look what it's brought us."

He pointed to the rats and the mouse. "It killed them and left them here. He brought me another one the night before last," Joel added.

Why had he confessed that when he had decided to say nothing? Now he would be punished, but receiving punishment was better than lying.

So Joel recounted Ta-Muit's midnight visit. Father was amazed. Then displeased. Then angry that the cat and its prey had violated the cleanliness of his home.

As Father spoke, Ta-Muit approached and rubbed its head against his bare calf. Father flinched away and kicked at the cat. His bare foot caught the animal in its belly and sent it flying toward the mud wall of the house across the street.

Ta-Muit screeched. So did Joel.

Then his mother and sister appeared at the door. "What is going on?" Mother exclaimed.

"A cat!" Miriam cried, delighted. "The one from the market?"

"Is she right, Nathan?" Mother asked. "It's really that cat?"

Father sighed. "Too true."

"Can I touch it?" Miriam wanted to know. She stepped toward Ta-Muit, whose eyes were fixed on her.

"No!" Mother warned. "It will bite you."

"No, it won't," Joel declared. He went to Ta-Muit and began petting him. Without warning, Miriam bounded across the street, sat down, and gathered the cat into her lap.

"Miriam!" Mother cried. "Get up! Joel, get that creature away from your sister."

He took Ta-Muit from Miriam and held the animal close. It squirmed, so he put it down again.

Mother looked at him suspiciously. "Joel, what do you know about all this?"

"It belongs to a child who was with the traders," Father explained. "Joel will tell us all about it."

He explained what had happened. In the meantime, Ta-Muit sat across the street, its eyes fixed on them.

Mother was horrified to learn that the animal had been in her house, and even more bothered to know about the dead rat. "I'll have to wash everything," she declared. "Your clothing, the blankets, the sleeping mats. You, Joel, will help me."

"But that's not man's work!" Joel protested. "Miriam can do it."

"Miriam didn't entertain a cat during the night and not tell us about it," Mother replied. "You should have awakened your father and me the second you knew that the animal had made its way inside."

"It was trying to help us," Joel insisted. "Father, you're always saying what a plague the rats and mice are. They chew holes in our sacks and eat our grain. Ta-Muit knows that! He wants to help us."

Father was skeptical. "So now you're as wise as King Solomon, who understands the actions of animals?" Father looked steadily at Joel, and his stern expression faded. There might even have been a bit of a smile in his eyes. "You say that 'he' wants to help us. But how do you know that this—animal is a male?"

Joel had assumed that Ta-Muit must be a boy, like himself. "I don't know," he replied.

"See if the cat will let you pick it up," Father instructed.

Joel did as he was told. Ta-Muit made no protest.

"Bring it here," Father said. "And let me see its back end." Then Father had a look. "The animal is a female, not a male."

"How do you know?" Miriam asked.

At that moment, Joel felt very much more grown up than his sister. *He* knew the difference—and how to tell.

"Your mother will explain it to you another time," Father said gently. "When you are a little older."

Meanwhile, Ta-Muit had begun to make that funny sound. Joel could not help but scratch *her* ears.

"Put her down," Father said. "She must go now."

"No, Papa!" Miriam exclaimed. "She wants to stay with us. She'll kill the bad rats and mice. She won't be any trouble."

Joel could have hugged his little sister. She was saying everything he himself wanted to say, and everyone in the family knew that Father had a hard time refusing his "Little Star."

Father hesitated. Then Mother sealed the cat's fate. "It will be all right, Nathan. How can we just turn away from this poor creature? Perhaps YAH himself has brought her to us. Can't we use a helper to keep away the terrible rats? Just think if a rat had gotten into our sleeping room and bitten one of the children? A cat will make rats think many times before they dare come into our house."

Father hugged Mother. Then he looked at Joel. Then he looked at Miriam, and a smile came over him.

"Please?" she begged.

Finally, Father reached out and put his hand on Ta-Muit herself. She raised her shoulders and stretched, as if to welcome his touch.

Everyone's eyes were fixed on Father, waiting for his decision.

"Very well," he said at last. "She—what is her name?"

"Ta-Muit," Joel reminded him.

"*Ta-Muit* can stay. We will not drive her away, and even if we did, I suspect this one would find her way back. But the animal must look to her own food. You children may give her water, but she is not to come into the house. She can find a place to sleep in the back garden. If Ta-Muit—what kind of nonsense name is that?— becomes a problem, then we will have to deal with her. Do you understand?"

Miriam threw her arms around her father's waist. "Thank you, Papa!" she cried. "Thank you."

"You are a good man, Nathan," Mother said.

"This is a mistake, Adah," he replied. "But what can a father do?"

Joel spoke a silent prayer to YAH for giving him the pet he had long been wanting, even without realizing it until yesterday.

Ten

Ta-Muit must have understood Father's decision, for she made herself completely at home from that moment.

Joel had a hard time concentrating on prayers that morning, for he wanted to see if the cat was still in the street nearby. But Ta-Muit seemed to have no intention of going far. Joel led her to the small garden back of the house and told her she could stay there. She followed him back to the street and proceeded to devour one of the rats she had killed. Miriam would not watch. Her feast completed, Ta-Muit carried the other rat and the dead mouse to the garden and placed them in a far corner where no onions or garlic grew. Mother gave her a pottery dish for water.

That evening, sleep was no friend to Joel. He knew he had to rest, and he tried, but he kept wondering about Ta-Muit and where she was sleeping. More troubling was this question: would she still be there in the morning?

She was. Two mice lay between her paws, both of them decapitated.

Mother needed olive oil for the morning meal, so first thing, she sent Joel and Miriam to Asher's shop. If they hurried, Joel could still arrive at school on time.

Ta-Muit decided she would go to the oil merchant, too.

As they made their way, neighbors immediately noticed their feline companion, and in a short while, several boys and girls were following them, Benjamin among them.

Joel and Miriam had to answer many questions.

"What is that?"

"A cat. Everyone knows that." Joel felt very superior.

"Where did it come from?"

"From the Egyptians traders."

"Why is it here? Why didn't it go with them?"

"It wanted to stay with us, and it did."

"But why?"

"Because it likes us."

"Does it bite?"

"It only bites people it *doesn't* like," Miriam said, knowingly.

Three children took quick steps away.

"Does it have a name?"

"Yes. Ta-Muit."

The cat perked up her ears when she heard that.

"What kind of dumb name is that?"

"Egyptian," Miriam replied. "Don't you know anything?"

"Is your father allowing it to stay with you?"

"Yes," Joel boasted.

"You must take it to King Solomon," Benjamin declared.

That idea had not occurred to Joel, and he didn't like it. "Why should I?"

"Everything belongs to the king. Maybe he'll want it."

"He has many animals already," Joel declared.

"But does he have a *cat*?" Benjamin asked.

"How should *I* know? Anyway, Ta-Muit came to *me*, not King Solomon."

"You think you're as good as the king?" someone asked.

Joel was beginning to feel annoyed. The other children had no business with Ta-Muit. But one thing was certain: her presence was no secret now. Soon, everyone In Jerusalem would know. Maybe the king himself would find out. Maybe he *would* summon Joel to the palace and claim Ta-Muit for himself.

No! That could not happen. YAH had given the cat to *him*—well, to be fair, to his family. King Solomon already had everything he could want. Besides, he was wise and good. He wouldn't seize an ordinary boy's pet. Would he?

As they went, Joel noticed grownups were staring. It had to be true: no one in Jerusalem had ever seen a real, live cat before. And now here was Ta-Muit: *his* pet.

At Asher's shop, Joel told the other children to wait in the street, or better yet, go on their way.

Asher greeted them warmly. "And who's this with you?" he asked.

"Ta-Muit," Miriam said. "She's our cat."

"Is she, now? And where did the little one come from?"

Ta-Muit went immediately to the man with the grizzled beard.

"She's friendly enough," he noted.

"She was with the traders," Joel told him. "They left, but she stayed. Now she's ours. Father says we can keep her."

Asher petted the cat. "I don't recall ever seeing another like her in Jerusalem. Our great king has his mighty cats, of course. Once he even possessed a leopard as black as ebony, but one morning, it was gone. No one ever discovered what had happened to it."

"Father says that Ta-Muit must feed herself," Joel added.

"Of course," Asher replied. "That's what cats do."

"How do you know?" Miriam asked.

"I was in Egypt once, a long time ago. Did you know that?"

They did not, so Asher told them about a journey many years earlier, when he was young—not so young as Joel, but not yet a man—and how he had run away with a caravan heading south. "I wanted to see the bigger world," he explained. "My parents were dead, and I was alone, so there was no one to worry when I was gone. I told a friend, and I promised I would return one day."

"And you did," Miriam said, quite sensibly.

Asher smiled. "Yes, I did. How else would I be here now?"

"Did you see cats in Egypt?" Joel asked.

"Oh, goodness, yes! The Egyptians love their cats as much as they love their beer, and that's saying a lot. Thousands of cats everywhere. You can't take three steps without stepping on a tail! Many earn their keep just as this one will do, by catching the rats and mice that feed on grain. There is so much grain in Egypt, pyramids of grain, more than you can imagine. Without cats, the rats would swallow it all."

"Did you see the stone pyramids?" Joel asked.

"Yes, I saw them. There are many, but three are the largest. They were built to be tombs for the pharaohs."

"Like the wicked pharaoh who would not let our people go?" Miriam asked.

"Very likely," Asher replied.

"I hate pharaohs."

Asher laughed. "How fierce you are, Miriam! The blood of Deborah must run in your veins."

"Tell us more about the cats of Egypt," Joel asked.

"Some wealthy Egyptians keep many cats as pets, and they don't make them find their own food. They provide them with delicacies better than you or I have ever imagined. Raw and cooked turtledoves. Fish from the great river. The eggs of herons and storks. And these cats, they eat from their masters' tables and sit underneath their masters' golden chairs and even sleep in their masters' beds!"

These wonders did not seem possible. But Asher had been there and seen them for himself.

"I suppose you know that the Egyptians worship a cat-headed goddess named Bastet," Asher continued. "And when cats die, they preserve their bodies and wrap them in strips of cloth and bury them in their own tombs with great ceremony."

"But why?" Joel asked.

"Because they say they are sacred to Bastet."

Joel was starting to understand why his father had been opposed to allowing Ta-Muit to stay.

"Don't worry," Asher assured them. "This one knows she is not a goddess. Just a friendly cat who's chosen a new home."

"*Chosen* a new home?" Miriam asked.

"Oh, yes," Asher told her. "People may think they are masters over cats, but I can tell you it's the other way around. Cats choose where they will live and how long they will stay, and whom they will love. They are not like dogs, who want masters. Cats have wild spirits."

"Do you mean Ta-Muit might leave us?" Miriam asked. "She just came!"

Asher looked thoughtful. "I can't say. But I do know this: treat her well. That's the best way to tempt her to stay. But if she decides to leave, don't take it too much to heart. Cats are like some people: they need to keep journeying, always curious about the next adventure. I think perhaps Ta-Muit wants to learn about our world here in Jerusalem. Let's hope she decides to make this her home. But if she determines to go, no cage can keep her."

Joel wasn't sure how to feel. He knew somehow that Asher was right, but he couldn't stand the thought that Ta-Muit might disappear someday. Not after she had chosen him! Well, he would do what Asher suggested: anything to make it so that Ta-Muit would want to stay—forever.

"Now what about that oil your mother sent you to get?" Asher asked.

The children gave him the empty vessels, and in a moment, they were filled with Asher's best oil. They paid him, and he gave them each a fig as a treat. For Ta-Muit, he had a morsel of dried goat meat. Then they headed back toward their home, the cat following close behind.

Eleven

Some of their friends were waiting for them when they came out of Asher's shop.

"Can I hold it?" Leah, Miriam's best friend, asked.

"No! She's mine."

"She's *mine*," Joel corrected her.

"She's *ours*," Miriam told Leah.

"Can we pet it, at least?" Benjamin wanted to know.

"It's not an 'it,'" Joel corrected him. "It's a she."

"Okay, then. Can we pet *her*?"

Joel didn't the see the point of being selfish. She *had* come to him as a kind of gift. "All right, if she'll let you."

Ta-Muit not only let the other children pet her, but also acted as if nothing in the world pleased her more than being the center of so much attention. Benjamin picked her up and the cat put a paw on his chin. "She likes me!" he exclaimed.

Joel let his friends have their moments with Ta-Muit but then realized he and his sister had been sent on an errand, and Mother would be impatient for the oil. Worse than that, he knew he was already late for school.

They hurried back home, a little parade of excited children of Jerusalem and one triumphant cat of Egypt, who had conquered a city without a sword, bow, or chariot.

Their friends dropped away one by one as Joel and Miriam approached their house.

"Where have you been?" Mother scolded. "You're already late," she told Joel. "Your father left here some time ago, and now you'll have to run to catch up. There's no time for your meal. Take this bread and eat it on your way."

"We were talking to Asher," Miriam explained. "He was in Egypt once."

"Good for Asher," Mother huffed. "It won't be good for you if you're one moment late," she warned Joel. She put a round loaf of flat bread in his hand. "Now run!" she commanded.

"Look after Ta-Muit," Joel called to Miriam as he dashed up the street. He arrived at school the very moment the other boys were settling onto their mats and arranging their tools. Elishama eyed him but said nothing. Breathless, Joel plopped down beside Benjamin.

"I wish I had a cat, too," was the first thing Benjamin whispered.

"She came to *me*," Joel whispered back. "Don't forget that."

Again, the day crawled on, more slowly than the desert tortoises that children sometimes brought into the city from the fields, and which their parents made them return just as quickly. Again, Joel's thoughts were outside, back at home, back to wherever Ta-Muit might be.

For the first time in his life, he hated what he was doing—or was being made to do. Just two days ago, he had been proud to be a scribe. Now, he felt like a prisoner. Worse—a slave.

Joel and Benjamin dashed out of school the moment Elishama dismissed the boys that afternoon. At home, all Joel's vague fears vanished when he found Ta-Muit curled up by the door, asleep in the sunshine. Joel touched her head, and she opened her eyes and stretched.

"Did you miss me?" he asked.

By way of answer, the cat yawned, showing her sharp, white teeth.

Joel smiled. "I guess not! Anyway, I'm home—if you care."

Ta-Muit licked a paw, rubbed her forehead, and settled back to her nap.

"Cats!" Joel grumbled.

Father came through the door. He must have gotten home before Joel. "She's still here. Your mother says that nosy neighbors have been stopping by all day to catch a glimpse."

"Do they like her?" Joel asked.

"I suppose. Your mother says that a few people muttered about cats having no business in Jerusalem—about cat worship in Egypt and such talk. I think everything will be all right. Anyway, it's no one else's business."

"You won't cause any trouble," Joel advised Ta-Muit.

"Not if she knows what's good for her," Father added. Then, "I'm going down to Jacob's house and help him repair a brick wall that's collapsed. I'd like you to come help."

That pleased him. Father had never asked for his help with jobs that required muscle instead of skill with a brush and ink. Besides, he'd rather be outside in the glow of late afternoon than cooped up in the house, helping Mother and Miriam with chores.

The collapsed wall had left sunbaked bricks lying in the street. It threatened to tumble down even more, so they would have to be careful. Jacob had no children of his own; in fact, his wife had died giving birth to his son, who also had died. That was a tragic loss, for children, especially sons, were highly valued in Israel.

Jacob was grateful for Father's and Joel's help. As they worked, Joel noticed how strong his father was. How had he gotten such muscular shoulders and arms while sitting inside copying dusty old papers and taking dictation?

Even though it was getting toward evening, the air was warm, and quickly Joel and the two other men were sweating. His arms began to ache, but he didn't want Father to know he was tiring. He kept moving dusty bricks to where no one would stumble over them. Jacob removed a brick from the wall and sure enough, many more came tumbling down. One hit him on the head.

"Are you all right?" Father asked.

Jacob shrugged. "It's nothing. I'm more embarrassed than hurt."

"Perhaps it did you a favor," Father remarked, his eyes twinkling.

Jacob picked up the offending brick and brushed the dust away. "How's that, Nathan?"

"By reminding you not to remove bricks from the bottom of a wall!"

Jacob laughed at Father's joke. Father joined him, and so did Joel. It felt good to be with other men working with his big muscles.

They labored until dusk, and then Father said it was time to be home for the evening meal. Jacob gave them water, and then he offered wine. Father drank from the wineskin, and then handed it to Joel. "A little," he said. "Too much wine is a mocker."

Joel felt proud to walk home beside his father. They talked about the day, about Joel's work, and Father's, and how the barley harvest was coming soon. That meant celebrating and offering of the first-fruits in the temple.

Ta-Muit was in the same place by the door.

"Still here?" Father asked. "We're going to have our meal soon. Perhaps you should go find yours."

Father was actually *talking* to the cat. Then he surprised Joel by reaching down and stroking her head. Ta-Muit got up, arched her back, as if asking for more. Now father was petting her!

Mother had the evening meal ready, and Joel ate more than usual, for working on the wall had made him extra hungry—and extra tired. He went to bed early, even before Miriam.

In the night, something touched his cheek. A fly, most likely. Half-awake, he brushed it away. Then it happened again. Again, he brushed it away. But as he fell back into sleep, it happened a third time. Only then was Joel awake enough to realize there was a weight on his chest. Startled, he moved to sit up. The weight lifted off him, and there was Ta-Muit sitting at his side!

"How did you get here?" Joel whispered.

A foolish question. *The same way you got here the other night,* he realized. But that didn't solve his problem.

"You can't be here!" he hissed.

By way of answer, Ta-Muit pawed his cheek again.

"You want to play," Joel said, keeping his voice as low as he could. Next to him, Miriam stirred. All was quiet from his parents' side of the room.

"I can't play now!" Joel whispered. "And you have to go."

He gathered Ta-Muit to himself, crawled to the ladder and began his way down. But he lost his footing and fell with a crash.

Ta-Muit screeched and leaped out of his arms, right onto a nearby table where Mother kept plates and bowls, which crashed onto the floor.

Laban and Dodo woke up and started bleating. Then Laban noticed the cat and began kicking at the sides of his stall to escape this strange creature that had invaded his space. He broke through and began thrashing about the room. He crashed into the water jars, which fell over and broke. Now there was water everywhere.

"What is going on?" Father shouted from upstairs. "Joel? What have you done?"

This is the end, Joel thought. *Father will kill Ta-Muit and I'll get a beating.*

"Nothing," Joel answered. "I just fell. I'm all right. I'll be right back up." That was a foolish thing to say. His back felt as though someone had struck him with a hundred bricks, but he could move, so at least he wasn't paralyzed. His right elbow, however, screamed with pain, and he knew he was bleeding.

"Don't tell me 'nothing,'" Father called. In a moment, he appeared, a lighted oil lamp in hand.

From the loft, Mother kept asking what was happening, and Miriam kept calling, "Papa?"

Father took in the scene of chaos. Laban kept blundering around the room, almost stepping on Joel, who hurt too much to try and move. Dodo did her part by bleating without stopping, and then she urinated. The acrid odor filled the room. Ta-Muit, terrified as well, pressed herself against the door, scratching frantically to be let out.

First, Father grabbed Laban and wrestled the animal back into its pen. Then he opened the door and Ta-Muit disappeared into the darkness outside.

Then he knelt beside Joel. "You *are* hurt," he said gently. "Can you sit up?"

Joel tried to push himself up, but the moment he put pressure on his right arm, the pain was so great he cried out.

Here came Mother and Miriam down the ladder. "Nathan, how bad is it?" Mother asked.

"I think he's broken a bone."

"Oh, no!" Mother exclaimed.

"Is Joel going to die?" Miriam asked. Then she began to cry.

"Of course not," Mother assured her. "He's going to be all right."

Mother held the oil lamp close while Father handled Joel's arm. No bone had broken through, and Joel could move his hand and fingers, which was a good sign, Father said. Nevertheless, each time Father moved Joel's arm in a certain way, the pain was terrible.

Mother brought Joel a bitter liquid and water to wash it down. "This will let you sleep," she promised.

Father half-carried him back up the ladder and helped him to lie down. He used a strip of cloth to tie the arm into a position where it didn't hurt so badly, and he said that in the morning, Joel would go to the physician. Now, there was nothing to do but try and rest.

When he had settled Joel, Father asked the question Joel had been expecting: "What happened with that cat? I know she's responsible for all this."

"She woke me by pawing my cheek. And she was sitting on my chest."

"How did she get in? Did you bring her inside?"

"No, sir! I don't know how she came in."

"The same way as the other night, I suppose. We can't board up the window. I don't know what to do, but one thing is certain: Ta-Muit makes trouble. She'll have to find another home, or—"

Joel couldn't allow his father to finish his thought. "I'll catch her and carry her outside the gates and let her loose in the fields! Then she won't be able to find her way back."

"She found her way here from the market," Father remarked.

"I know, but—"

Father put a finger to Joel's mouth. "No more talk tonight. We'll solve this in the morning, *after* we clean up the mess and take you to the physician. Rest now."

Mother sat down next to him. She began stroking his hair and sang softly to him.

"You sang that to me when I was little," Miriam said. "To make me sleep."

"Indeed I did," Mother told her.

"But Joel isn't little."

"No, he's a young man now. But he still needs to rest, and this song always works."

With Mother's lullaby in his ears, Joel fell asleep.

Twelve

Mother and Miriam began to clear away the mess from the disaster of the night before. Laban and Dodo were more than glad to be released into Issachar's care, so their stall was mucked out and fresh straw put down. Mother worked to prepare the morning meal, but all the broken dishes made it difficult. She remarked that a visit to the potter would be necessary later that morning.

Joel remained in the loft room, waiting for Father to help him down the ladder. His arm throbbed, and he felt groggy from the medicine Mother had given him. Also, he needed to use the latrine so badly that he could scarcely hold it. Father brought him a chamber pot. He hated that. Pots were for little children, and he hadn't used one in some years. It was embarrassing.

There was no sign of Ta-Muit, who was certainly gone forever. That thought, plus his pain and guilt for all the trouble he'd caused, made him feel like crying. In fact, he did cry silently so that no one would hear him behaving like a baby.

After a while, Father helped him down the ladder, and the family ate. No one spoke a word of blame.

Father sent Miriam to Benjamin's house with the message that Joel had broken his arm and would not be in school. Benjamin would tell Elishama, and Father would stop by later to let him know what the physician had said.

The physician lived only a few streets away. He examined Joel's right forearm. When he manipulated the bone, Joel's pain was severe. Father put his hand under Joel's left hand and told him to squeeze as hard as he could. Somehow, that helped.

The physician worked with the bone until satisfied it was back in its right position. It didn't take long, but Joel had to clench his teeth to keep from screaming again. Once the bone was in place, the physician brought out some thin pieces of wood and strips of cloth to fashion a splint. He also produced a small amulet of faience shaped to look like a forearm with a small hand at one end. He intended to place it among the wrappings. "It will protect your son from evil and speed his healing," the physician promised. "The power of YAH works through it."

Father agreed. He helped by holding the wood in place while the physician began wrapping Joel's arm tightly. After he'd circled the arm three times, he asked Father to hold the amulet in place until it was secured under the next layer of cloth. Soon, the work was done.

"How does it feel?" he asked.

"It still hurts, but not as badly," Joel told him. He moved his fingers, and the pain got worse. The moment he stopped, it was better.

"How long will he need this?" Father asked.

"Young ones heal quickly," the physician promised.

Joel didn't like being called a "young one."

"How long?" Father repeated. "My son goes to the school for scribes, and his teacher will want to know."

The physician nodded. "Writing will be impossible until the splint is no longer needed. Even then, as the bone heals, your son will have to be careful not to strain it. He may not be able to return to his school for some weeks."

Father looked concerned, but Joel felt glad. Not to have to go to school! Not to have to copy!

It if weren't for the pain, he was glad his arm was broken. The moment he thought that, he knew how wicked he was. Glad that he had fallen down the ladder and created such a problem for his family? Glad that he couldn't continue his training, when it was so important for his life?

Then another thought came to him. Ta-Muit had made all this possible! He would thank *her* for his time away from school. Thank her, that is, if she ever returned.

Father paid the physician, who spoke the blessing of YAH over them and told them to return in a week so that he could inspect the injury and renew the splint.

Joel felt miserable. His arm ached, and he was exhausted from not having slept well. Furthermore, it was his cat's fault that so many dishes were broken and Father would have to buy new ones.

And he would certainly never see Ta-Muit again.

At home, Father helped him back up the ladder. He brought the chamber pot, and Mother offered water, bread, and some dried fruit. "Now rest," she told him. "It will help you to heal."

Part of Joel didn't like being treated like a little child, but another part enjoyed being pampered—like a little child! He found a comfortable position on his mat, and immediately fell asleep.

When he woke up, it was the middle of the day. His injured arm ached, and he asked Mother to give him more of her medicine. She did, and he slept again until he heard his father talking downstairs. It sounded as though he was arguing with someone. The other voice was at first unfamiliar, but then Joel recognized it: his grandfather, Eliezer, a priest of YAH. Why were their voices angry? Joel crept to the opening in the floor and listened.

"And what was a *cat* doing in your home in the first place?" His grandfather was almost shouting.

"I told you, Father. It somehow found its way into the house and was bothering Joel in the middle of the night."

That wasn't exactly true, so why would Father say so?

Joel called down to the room below. "She was just visiting me, Grandfather. She wasn't bothering me."

"Come down," Grandfather commanded. "I need to talk to you."

"I'll help him," Father said. He climbed the ladder and when his head appeared, Joel could see how irritated he was. "Why did you contradict me?" he whispered furiously. "Now you've made me out to be a liar in front of my own father."

"But it didn't happen that way," Joel whispered back.

"Come down!" Grandfather ordered.

Father shook his head in exasperation. No wonder. Everyone knew that Joel's grandfather considered himself always right about any subject that came up. He once said he didn't hate losing an argument because he never *had* lost one. So how could he know how that would feel?

Joel came down. His arm, which had been feeling all right, began to throb. It came to him that he should act like he was badly hurt. Maybe that would gain his grandfather's sympathy.

Downstairs, Joel found his grandfather standing in the middle of the room as if he were master of the house. Mother stood to one side, and Miriam clung to her skirts. She loved her grandfather, as Joel did, but she was a little afraid of him, too—as Joel was.

He knew what to do. He went to the old man, who was even taller than his father, his beard long and gray but neatly trimmed, his eyebrows thick and black. Joel nodded in respect. "Grandfather, may the blessing of YAH be upon you."

"YAH bless and keep you, my son," Grandfather replied. Then he got down to business. "What are these tales I hear of an *Egyptian cat* taking up residence in this house?" He said "Egyptian cat" as if it were a foul thing.

Joel explained, starting with the traders and the boy Seb. He told of Ta-Muit's gifts of rats and mice, and how he had never brought the animal into the house himself. Somehow, she had found her own way.

"And the animal came to the loft and was about to harm you when you woke up and tried to carry it down the ladder so you could cast it into the street?"

Joel caught his father's eye. He had to be careful about what he said. "I don't think she was going to bite me, if that's what you mean."

Grandfather gave Father an accusing look. "You suggested the animal was attacking the boy."

"I said 'bothering' him. Maybe I was mistaken," Father replied.

Grandfather shook his head. "Or maybe you still have trouble telling the truth! That was your failing when you were a boy, and it appears that you have not grown out of it."

"Father—"

"I lied," Joel volunteered. "I told Father Ta-Muit was going to hurt me. I woke up and saw her staring at me. She looked into my eyes, and I thought she was trying to put me under a spell." The moment the words were out, Joel realized how foolish they must sound.

But Grandfather looked grave. "Quite possibly," he agreed. "Egyptian deviltry. You were right to rid the house of that evil creature, but you should have awakened your parents to help you. Now look at what your foolish pride has caused. A broken arm. The loss of your mother's dishes. The cost of a physician. I hope you have learned your lesson. YAH does not overlook sin!"

Mother saved the day. "We thank you for your wisdom, Father-in-Law," she soothed. "We have spoken severely to the boy about his wrongdoings, and he has promised that his dealings with the cat are now at an end."

That was not strictly true, either. Joel could recall no such conversation. He only assumed that Ta-Muit was gone for good, after the disaster she had caused. But Grandfather looked less angry, and another fight between him and Joel's father had been averted.

"Let me see your arm," Grandfather asked Joel. His voice was calm now.

Joel held out his arm.

"What does the physician say?"

Father answered. "He was able to set the bone back into its correct place. It should heal well. Until it does, Joel should not do any copying."

"He put an amulet among the wrappings to help it heal faster," Joel added.

"What?" Grandfather exclaimed. "He did *what*?"

"An amulet—"

"Idolatry!" Grandfather thundered. He turned on Joel's father. "Did you know of this?"

"Of course! I was there the whole time."

"And you let him put a heathenish spellbinder against the body of a child of YAH?"

"All the physicians in Jerusalem use such aids," Father shot back. "What's the harm?"

"I would expect to find such abominations in Philistine temples! Among the potions and spells of Egyptian magicians! Not in Jerusalem. Do you not trust in our god to heal your son, or must you mix the faith of our people with the corrupt practices of our enemies?"

Grandfather was shouting. Miriam, wide-eyed, began to whimper.

"There's no need for such anger," Father said. "Please stop. You're frightening the child."

"She should be *more* frightened to live in a house where cats are free to roam, bringing with them the contagions of Egypt. Where a son of Abraham bears a pagan charm on his body because his parents do not trust in the healing power of their own god!"

"That's enough," Father said. Joel could tell he was trying hard to contain his rage. It would never do to speak harshly to one's father, especially when he was a priest.

"What you are allowing here is *more* than enough," the older man shot back. "Unwrap the boy's bandages," he commanded.

"I will not," Father declared.

"Then I will! Hold out your arm," he ordered Joel.

Joel looked to his father, then his mother, hoping they would tell him what to do. For a moment, no one spoke or moved. The only sound in the room was that of Miriam's whimpering.

"I am head of this house," Father said at last. His voice was low but solid as Mt. Zion. "I decide whether my son may befriend an animal, even a cat of the Egyptians. I decide what treatment he receives for his broken bone, including whether to permit the physician to use a healing amulet. This is my house, Father, and I ask you to respect me as its head."

Grandfather stood silent and astonished. Joel could see him breathing hard, even though he was wearing a long robe that covered him from his neck to his sandaled feet.

Everyone remained motionless, waiting for the storm to break.

Thirteen

But when Grandfather spoke, it was with words just as quiet—and as firm—as his son's. "You were ever headstrong and disobedient, Nathan, from the time you were younger than your own son here. You were raised to take your rightful place among the priests of YAH and to devote your life to service in His temple. But you denied your heritage. You turned away from a privilege that many men in Israel long to enjoy. And for what? To spend your life making scratches on scraps of papyrus! To copying lists of goods bought and sold. 'Ten omers of barley! Seven ephahs of oats! Ten baths of oil.' Bah! Nothings compared to the joy of raising prayers to YAH. To offering sacrifices. To serving in his house. You are wasting your life on trifles, so I should not be surprised when you allow your family to trifle with heathenish things such as cats and amulets. I will pray for you." Grandfather glanced at Mother, at Miriam, and then at Joel. "For all of you."

"Father—"

Grandfather held up a hand. "Enough. I have spoken. Now let me go before more hurtful words are said." With that, he turned and left without a farewell blessing—without a word.

Father's head was bowed and his eyes closed. His fists were clenched.

"Nathan?" Mother asked.

"Nothing ever changes. Everything I do is wrong. I will never be able to please him."

"That's not true," Mother said. "He loves you. And he respects you. And—perhaps—he envies your ability to read and write."

"If he respects me, he has a strange way of showing it. To speak to me like that—in front of . . . "

Father looked at Miriam and then at Joel. "Forgive me, children, for answering disrespectfully to your grandfather. When we are both calmer, I will beg his forgiveness."

"This is all my fault," Joel whispered.

"No, son," Father countered.

"It is," Joel insisted. "If I hadn't made friends with Ta-Muit, I wouldn't have fallen and hurt my arm. You wouldn't have had to take me to the physician. There would be no amulet on me."

"Do you want me to remove it?" Father asked.

Joel looked into his father's eyes, and there he saw much pain, but also his father's love. "Yes, sir."

"Let me do it," Mother said. "Outside, where there's light." Mother held Joel's arm in her lap and unwrapped the bandages. Miriam stood close by, fascinated.

"Nothing bad is underneath," Mother promised her. "Just a tiny bit of dried clay." In a moment, the amulet appeared. Mother picked it up and inspected it. "Harmless," she declared.

"Father is set in his ways," Father added.

Mother smiled ruefully. "As we've known for a long time. Since your mother died, he's become more and more unyielding. It's sad."

"Let me have that," Father asked. Mother gave him the amulet, and Father crushed it underfoot. "Now let's hope my father will be satisfied."

Mother rewrapped Joel's arm. She did it just as well as the physician had done, maybe even better. Then she kissed Joel's cheek. "I'm sorry for all this upset. Are you tired? Do you want to rest again?"

"I'm all right."

"Then how about taking a walk with me?" Father asked.

"Go," Mother urged Joel. "Some fresh air will make you feel better."

Joel and his father set out. "Let's not go up toward the temple," Father advised. "We don't want to encounter your grandfather again—not just yet."

Joel had many questions, but Father needed to talk, too.

"I'm sorry you saw me quarrel with your grandfather," he began. "He and I have never seen things the same way, and that's been hard for us both. Many times I've broken YAH's commandment about honoring parents, and many times I've asked my father's forgiveness. Many times he has given it. That's how I know how much he loves me."

They walked toward the market. People they knew spoke to them, greeting Father with the usual respect. It didn't seem possible that a good man such as he would ever have broken YAH's commandments or would have had so many battles with his own father.

"You were supposed to be a priest?" Joel asked. He had never known that.

"Yes," Father admitted. "It was your grandfather's great desire for me. Not many men in Israel can hope for such an honor. But it wasn't right for me. I am too . . . "

"Too what?"

"Rebellious, your grandfather would say. Headstrong. Determined to go my own way. Perhaps he's always been right. I don't know. But I *do* know how much hurt I've caused him. It makes me ashamed."

Joel had never heard his father talk like this. He felt shaky inside, as if he'd opened a door to a room full of secrets too big to understand.

This was the first time his father was speaking to him as a man speaks to another man, about the hurts and sadness of life. Yes, his grandfather must be lonely in his house, especially at night. Father must be sad when he stopped to think that by choosing to go his own way, he had hurt his father, whom he loved.

Joel could find no words. Instead, not caring who noticed, he took his father's hand. That's how they walked through the lower city, circled back, and came to their own house.

Fourteen

Joel was so tired that he went to his sleeping mat just after the evening meal. Mother gave him another dose of her medicine. He slept immediately and was awakened next morning by his father's voice calling from the room below. "Joel, someone has left you a gift at the door!"

Joel crawled to the opening in the loft floor and looked down. "What is it?"

"Two rats and three mice. The mice have no heads."

"Ta-Muit!" Joel exclaimed. This was the first good thing to happen since he fell down the ladder. "Is she here?"

"I don't see her anywhere. I looked in the street and walked to the garden. No sign of her."

"I want to come down," Joel said.

By this time, Mother and Miriam were awake. Father helped Joel down and then sent him and his sister to the latrine. Joel's arm was feeling better, so in a few days, he knew he could return to school. That thought gave him no pleasure, however.

Joel spent another day at home, mostly resting. He figured a way to get up and down the ladder using only his good arm, and he drowsed through the morning and afternoon while Mother and Miriam took care of the house.

Father came home and said he had not seen Grandfather, which was likely just as well. Father also said that Elishama had asked about Joel and hoped he would soon rejoin the class.

Issachar returned, as usual, with Laban and Dodo. That gave Joel an idea.

"Since I can't go back to school, may I go with Issachar tomorrow? Father, you said I could one day."

Father looked to Mother, who nodded. "I don't see why not. Just remember to guard your arm. You don't want to injure it again."

That's how it was decided. The next morning when Issachar arrived, Joel was ready. He was happy to see a rat, a mouse, and a bat at the doorstep; Ta-Muit was somewhere nearby, perhaps calculating when she would be welcome back. In the meantime, she was bringing peace offerings.

Mother put food in a sling pouch so Joel would have something for the mid-day meal. She offered a lot of advice about being careful, and Miriam kept asking why she couldn't go, too. Father blessed both boys.

As they made their way up the street toward the eastern gate, others joined them. Shepherds, farmers, brickmakers, repairers of roads, even some soldiers whose job it was to keep guard near the fields and pastures, mostly as a warning to bandits stay away.

Once outside the gates, Issachar led the way toward the open fields and rocky pastures. Joel had been beyond the walled city a few times, but except for Sukkot, when families lived eight days in shelters to remember their ancestors' wanderings before entering the Promised Land, he could not recall spending an entire day outside.

As if to repay him for his lifelong absence, this day was perfect. The air was cool, and the wind blew gently. Overhead, the sun shone like fire in a field as blue as the lapis lazuli inlays on the walls of King Solomon's palace. Overhead, migrating birds continued their pilgrimage songs.

Joel felt like dancing just as wildly as Seb had whirled that night in the market. He felt like shouting. Like spreading wide his arms to embrace the whole world outside of the prison-like walls and narrow, dull streets of Jerusalem. He looked at Issachar and envied him. No wonder his friend was bigger and stronger than himself. No wonder his skin was browner, his fair hair lightened from living out beneath the sun day after day.

The two boys walked at the head of Issachar's flock. All around them, people were starting the day's work in field and pasture and olive grove. They saw men beginning a long day building a new stone wall. Children gathered fallen sticks beneath ancient olive trees. In the golden fields of ripening barley, women labored to clear away weeds. Shepherds kept on their way, heading for the higher ground where it was too rocky for crops, but green enough for sheep.

It took a good long while to arrive at the pasture. Issachar greeted his brothers, who had spent the night with their sheep. One of them, Gaddiel, would now return to the city to rest. He had been charged with keeping watch while Hamor, Issachar's other brother, had slept. Issachar brought food for Hamor, as well as a skin of water.

Gaddiel didn't say much. In fact, he looked grumpy. When Issachar asked him what was wrong, he muttered something about being sick of living like an animal and that he wished he could find another profession.

Hamor seized his meal and ate greedily. "You're the son of Nathan ben-Eliezer," he noted.

"Yes, sir," Joel said.

"What'd you do to your arm?"

"I broke it."

"How?"

"Fell down the ladder in my house."

"That was clumsy," Hamor declared.

The man did not have good manners. He looked like a ruffian, too, with long stringy hair, an unkempt beard, soiled tunic, and an odor like—sheep.

"You know Joel," Issachar reminded his brother.

"I just called him by name, didn't I?"

"Sort of. His family lives just down the street from us."

Hamor grunted. "What's your point? I'm not in the city often enough to keep up with my neighbors. We shepherds are doomed to live up here, without baths and barbers and launderers."

"Mother would cut your hair," Issachar reminded him. "And wash your clothes if you ever changed them. You could get a bath, too—if you wanted one."

"And how's it your business, what I do?"

"It's not, except that the rest of us have to smell you."

Joel laughed, but Hamor was not amused.

"You good-for-nothing!" he exclaimed. He threw a date at his brother. Issachar dodged, and the sheep dog, Gideon, who had not taken his eyes off Hamor's meal for one second, instantly snapped it up.

"Lead your pitiful flock to the upper pasture and don't let me see your face until evening," Hamor ordered.

"I was only joking, brother," Issachar replied. "Don't be angry."

Hamor grumbled something about how no one respected him and that when he escaped Jerusalem one day, all his family would miss him. But then, it would be too late for their regrets.

"Come on," Issachar told Joel. "We'll have to come back before evening and water the animals one last time. In the meantime, I've got plenty for us right here." He patted the skin slung over his shoulder. "And you've brought food, too."

"Mother packed enough for us both."

Issachar grinned. "You should come with me every day!"

Issachar whistled, and Gideon got to his work. He circled the herd, nipped here, nudged there, and in a moment had the sheep moving up the hill toward higher ground. When they arrived, Issachar waved back to Hamor, whose piercing whistle summoned the dog to return. The sheep dispersed, seeking grass, and Issachar and Joel put their provisions by a ramshackle wall of stone, about as high as Joel's waist. It was part of an old sheep pen, long abandoned.

Joel didn't want to sit. He wanted to roam, to explore. All around him was life. Yellow and white butterflies, buzzing blue flies. Red poppies, white anemones, and purple bellflowers. And grass, still tender and pale green in the early spring sunshine.

Was the Garden of Eden as beautiful as this? Joel wondered.

In the distance, the city gleamed in the sunlight. They could see it glinting from the tops of the two pillars on either side of the temple doors, and from the enormous bronze sea that stood in the courtyard. Joel could pick out King Solomon's palace and from there guessed which building was his school. But his house was impossible to locate in the maze of streets and identical flat-roofed dwellings. Up here, atop the highest hill, no two things were exactly alike—no two stones, no two lizards scurrying for cover lest they be trampled by sheep, not even any two poppies.

The boys talked. They picked up stones and threw them, trying to hit a scrubby bush nearby. Issachar had a good arm and a keen eye. Joel couldn't use his right arm, of course, and he was clumsy with his left. Still, it felt good to exercise his legs and arm. He found himself breathing hard, and his face and neck were damp with sweat.

The sheep settled into one area and began grazing. The boys sat in the sun for a while, then found shade beside another ruined wall. They drank from the water skin.

"How about some fresh milk?" Issachar asked.

"That sounds good. Where will we get it?"

Issachar gave Joel a look that said, "Are you as dumb as the question you just asked?"

Joel laughed at himself. They were surrounded by sheep, including ewes. Issachar chose one that was most gentle. He told Joel how to hold her head, and Issachar milked her into a pottery bowl he brought out of his shepherd's bag.

They drank, and it tasted more delicious than anything else Joel had ever tasted—warm, sweet, and smelling faintly of grass and wildflowers.

"Can I try?" he asked.

"Of course! It's not difficult, but you have to be firm and gentle at the same time. You'll figure it out soon enough."

It was not as simple as Issachar made it sound, and the ewe, recognizing unskilled hands, was restless. Nevertheless, Joel managed, and before long, they had another bowlful of milk. He had the makings of a shepherd.

Fifteen

THE morning passed in peace. Joel drowsed. When he couldn't keep his eyes open, Issachar told him to rest; it was no problem for him to watch the sheep alone. Joel spread his cloak on the ground in the shade of the broken wall and instantly slept.

The next thing he knew, Issachar was shaking his left shoulder. "Wake up! Wake up, Joel!"

"What's wrong?" he asked groggily.

"You have to see this!"

He sat up and looked to where Issachar was pointing.

Ta-Muit was sitting by the wall, about three cubits from him.

"Ta-Muit!" he exclaimed. "Where did you come from? What are you doing here? I thought you were gone forever."

"It's mid-day," Issachar explained. "I just came back to see if you were all right. I found it—" he pointed to the cat—"sitting right there, as if she'd been watching over you. I went to her, and I thought she'd run from me, but she didn't. Then I noticed it."

"Noticed what?"

"Look for yourself."

Joel walked toward Ta-Muit. She didn't move but kept her eyes on him. Then he saw what Issachar was talking about: between the cat's paws was the torn body of a dead snake.

"An asp!" Issachar exclaimed. "One bite, and you'd be dead. The cat killed it to protect you!"

Joel felt a shiver run down his back. Was it true? Had Ta-Muit saved his life? That was a question with no sure answer. Another was this: how had Ta-Muit found her way out of the city, through the fields, up into the hills, and right to where Joel and Issachar were tending the flock?

Joel squatted in front of the cat. "*Did* you kill it to protect me?" he asked.

Ta-Muit pawed at the dead creature, which looked to be more than a cubit long. Joel knew about poisonous snakes; one bite from this one, and he would have died a terrible death.

"You!" he exclaimed, rubbing his hand across Ta-Muit's head. She stretched her neck under his touch, and then she let him—and Issachar—pet her. He had never touched a cat before, just as Joel had never milked a ewe.

"Where have you been?" Joel asked the cat. "And how did you find me?"

"YAH sent her to protect you," Issachar declared. "He must hold you in great favor to save you from the asp."

"Do you really think so? Why should he? I'm nobody important."

"YAH's ways are mysterious. Ta-Muit is here to watch over you."

Joel shook his head. "I don't understand any of this."

"Bring her home this evening," Issachar suggested. "We'll take the asp as proof how she murdered it to save your life."

That was a good idea. After he heard how Ta-Muit had protected his son, Father would have to let her stay. Perhaps even allow her inside the house.

Ta-Muit remained with the boys all the rest of the afternoon. For a while, they lay on their backs and watched the clouds while she napped nearby. The sheep moved from place to place among the hills, and Issachar led them to a drinking trough. Then they came to a level place where the ground was sandy, with few rocks. Joel smoothed a place with his hand, and then he began to draw with his left index finger. He drew a sheep, then a gorse bush growing nearby. Ta-Muit came along, sat near him, and Joel drew her.

"You're good," Issachar praised. "Where'd you learn how to do that?"

"Nowhere. A few days ago, at school, I started to draw on my papyrus. The master didn't like it, and I got in trouble."

"Because you weren't doing your assigned work?"

"I guess so, but Elishama said that being able to write words is better than being able to draw pictures."

"What's wrong with drawing pictures? The Egyptians do it. I've seen their scrolls when they come through town."

"Father says those scrolls are evil, and the pictures on them represent false gods. They're full of spells, too, and one of them is supposed to tell how dead people can be resurrected!"

"That's not true," Issachar scoffed. "If it were, then everybody in Egypt would live forever. When someone died, they'd just read the magic spell over them, and they'd come back to life. Think about it, Joel. It's not possible." What Issachar said made sense. Not everything people told you was true. But did that include his father? And his grumpy grandfather?

"Draw me," Issachar said.

"No! Why?"

"Afraid YAH is going to strike you down?"

"No . . . "

"What, then?"

"Nothing!"

"Then do it—if you can."

They were alone, a long way from Hamor and his flock. Joel looked down the hills to the valley, where he could see people—tiny people—busy in the fields. There was no one to see him draw—not his father, not his grandfather, not Elishama.

But YAH would see, wouldn't He?

"What are you waiting for?" Issachar challenged. "You're just scared."

"Am not!"

"Then do it. I'll sit still."

Joel couldn't let Issachar think he was frightened, even though he was nervous. Besides, there was no harm drawing in the sand, and no one else would ever know.

"All right," Joel agreed.

Drawing a sheep or a cat was one thing, but a person was harder. Joel had to smooth things over and start again once or twice, and then he had to make the nose longer, the eyes farther apart, the chin squarer, the ears smaller. Issachar stayed still, and he didn't talk.

At last, the work was done. "You can look now," Joel said.

Issachar gave the dirt drawing a long, serious look.

"Well?" Joel asked.

"It's all right, I guess. Does it look like me?"

"Don't you know?"

"How would I? I can't see my own face."

"You've never looked in a mirror?"

"Have you?"

"No. Mother doesn't own one, and Grandfather says that they tempt a person to the sin of vanity."

"What's vanity?"

"Thinking you're more handsome or beautiful than you really are and doing things to make yourself look better. Like the way the Egyptians draw around their eyes with kohl and wear fancy wigs and all that jewelry."

"I saw one of their mirrors once," Issachar remembered. "At the market. It was made of polished bronze, and the handle was a naked woman!"

"Did you touch it?"

Issachar looked embarrassed. "Yes. The merchant offered it to me, and I held it in front of my face. I could see myself a little, but not very well."

"Did you think you were handsome?"

"Of course! If I looked that good in the mirror, I can only imagine how great I look in person!"

"Vanity!" Joel joked. "I'd better scratch this out so you don't commit such a sin."

"Is that how I really am?"

"Yes. Actually, the picture looks better than you do."

Issachar grabbed Joel and held him down. They scuffled.

"My arm!" Joel protested. "Watch out for my arm, you big bully!"

"You deserve a beating, you liar!" Issachar threatened. "Take back what you said!" He was trying to sound serious, but he started to laugh. Joel joined him.

Issachar let him up, and the boys sat side by side, panting and joking. The drawing was gone, obliterated as they wrestled. Joel couldn't remember a day he'd enjoyed more than this one.

When it was time to go, Ta-Muit approached and took her place between them.

"Take the asp with you," Issachar reminded Joel. "Proof for why your cat has got to stay with you."

Joel found the snake, which was already being eaten by ants. He prodded it to make sure it was really dead. Then he picked it up by its tail and shook off the ants.

"I'll put it in my pouch," Issachar offered. Joel didn't object.

Off they went. The sheep seemed not even to notice Ta-Muit's presence, or if they did, they gave no sign.

Soon enough, they came to Hamor and his flock. The faithful Gideon was on the lookout; no danger could come near without his giving warning. He spied Ta-Muit and began to bark. The cat, for her part, puffed up the hair on her back and growled.

Hamor gave no greeting, nor did he seem pleased or even interested to see them back. "What's that?" he asked, nodding at Ta-Muit.

"A cat, as if you didn't know."

"Where'd it come from?"

"The Egyptian traders left it in town, and it's Joel's cat now."

"Says who?"

"Says my father," Joel declared.

"It killed an asp that was about to bite Joel while he slept," Issachar asserted.

"Yeah? How do you know that? Did you see her do it?"

"No, but look." Issachar produced the dead asp from his bag.

"A big one," Hamor said. "And the cat killed it."

"That's what I said!"

“But you didn’t see it happen.”

“No, but what else could have done it? Not one of the sheep.”

Hamor examined the dead snake. “It’s been bitten through the neck, and there *are* claw marks all over it. I guess you’re telling the truth. Joel’s cat killed a snake.”

Meanwhile, Gideon and Ta-Muit had moved warily closer to one another. Then the dog sniffed the cat, who pawed him none too lightly on the end of his nose. Gideon looked surprised, but he let the insult pass. In a few moments, the two animals were friends. Ta-Muit sealed the deal by rubbing against Gideon’s front right leg, and Gideon licked her head.

“The cat’s coming home with Joel to stay with him all the time because she’s his protector,” Issachar informed his brother.

“That so? Nice for Joel.”

"You’re just jealous.”

“Of what?”

“Of not having a cat of your own.”

Hamor rolled his eyes. “What would I do with a cat? I’ve got more than enough animals to take care. If anyone’s jealous, it’s you, little brother.”

“Come on,” Issachar told Joel. “You can’t have a civil conversation with a shepherd.”

“You’re one, too!” Hamor exclaimed. “Don’t forget it.”

“As if I could,” Issachar said.

“If you see our worthless brother, tell him to hurry up. I’m starving.”

“See you later,” Issachar said.

“Go with YAH, cat boy,” Hamor called after Joel.

Joel wasn’t sure to be angry with Hamor or to laugh at him. “May YAH bless you,” he called back.

“He’s not a bad fellow,” Issachar said. “Just half-wild.”

Joel couldn’t help wondering what it *would* be like, living in the open hills. It could be dangerous, with asps, scorpions, lions, and even bears. And robbers out to steal sheep. And having to keep constant watch over them so they wouldn’t wander away and get lost. Or fall off a cliff. Or the ewes having trouble delivering their lambs and needing the shepherds to put their hands into their wombs and pull the babies out. That wouldn't be pleasant.

But then there was the sky. The fields of grain, the vineyards, and the groves of olive and pomegranate trees. The upland pastures with their carpets of wildflowers. And the golden sunshine.

Hamor might complain about his life, but at the moment it felt preferable to sitting indoors, legs crossed, one's nose to a piece of papyrus, copying endless lists, afraid of making mistakes. Taking dictation, hoping to hear the speaker's words correctly, writing as fast as one could in order to keep up . . .

Such a life was not fun. And it was not for Joel. One day in the pastures with Issachar had convinced him. He, Joel, would have a different life from the one his father had planned for him.

There were just two problems:

How would he break that news to his father?

Then, how would he persuade Father to let him take a different way—*his own way*?

Sixteen

The boys attracted a lot of attention as they made their way back toward the city. By now, some people in Jerusalem must have heard about an Egyptian cat rumored to have taken up residence in the house of Nathan ben-Eliezer. Only a few had seen Ta-Muit, though, and now they were discovering that the rumors were true.

Children returning from their days' work crowded to see the cat. The old jealousy came over Joel: Ta-Muit was *his*, no one else's, not even Miriam's. He was glad when they arrived at home. Issachar gave Joel the dead asp and then went his way, saying he hoped Joel could join him again tomorrow.

Mother was surprised to see Ta-Muit back, and Miriam was overjoyed. She begged that she be let inside the house, but Mother refused, reminding Miriam that Father had forbidden it. So she sat on the bench by the door, proudly displaying Ta-Muit to everyone who came along.

Joel showed Mother the asp, and she was properly horrified. "I knew I shouldn't have let you go with Issachar," she exclaimed.

Had he just doomed any chance to spend more days up in the high hills? "I was in no danger," he tried to explain.

"No danger? Do you see what it is you've brought into the house? Please take it away. Bury it in the garden! The sight of it makes me go cold."

"Ta-Muit was there to protect me," Joel insisted. "YAH sent her to do that."

"We'll see what your father has to say."

At that moment, Father came through the door. "Say about what?" he asked. "And where did that wretched cat come from? Miriam's outside announcing that the animal is staying with us forever."

Mother pointed to the offending carcass. "Your son was sleeping in the pasture today and this—*thing* was about to bite him when the cat attacked and killed it."

Father gave Joel the skeptical look he knew all too well.

"It's true!" Joel exclaimed. "Issachar says that YAH sent Ta-Muit to protect me."

"So now Issachar's a prophet? You're completely certain of that?"

"Not completely," he admitted. "But maybe! We don't know how Ta-Muit found us in the pasture, and she *did* kill this snake, which was close to me—"

"Or she killed it somewhere else and brought it to you, the way she does with rats and mice."

"I can't say for certain," Joel admitted. "But I believe the snake was coming to bite me, and Ta-Muit saw I was in danger, and she killed it to save me."

"And I want her to stay with us *in the house* now," added Miriam, coming through the door, Ta-Muit clutched in her arms.

"And why is that, Little Star?"

"Because I love her!"

Father and Mother laughed. "I see that you do," Father said. "You love her so much that you're squeezing the life out of her."

Miriam put the cat down. "I'm sorry!" she cried. "I don't want to squish you."

Ta-Muit, who always seemed to know just what to do, walked directly to Father and looked at him.

"All right!" Father said. "She may stay as long as she likes."

"Inside?" Joel asked.

"Inside. I suppose we can't refuse a cat sent by YAH to protect us."

Miriam grabbed Father's leg. "Thank you, Papa! Thank you!"

"Can she sleep with us?" Joel asked, certain that his father would say no.

But he didn't. "I suppose. But the first night she keeps me awake is the night she goes back outdoors."

"I hope she doesn't snore the way you do," Mother teased Father. "Then the rest of us truly will have no prayer of getting a night's rest!"

"I don't snore that much—" Father tried to protest.

Everyone else's laughter made him decide not to push the point.

And so Ta-Muit joined the family.

Joel's arm felt a little better each day. The physician examined him, wondered what had happened to the amulet, and said nothing when Father explained that they removed it and decided to trust in YAH for healing.

"When you can use your brush without pain, you should think of returning to school, but not for an entire day," the physician advised them. "Only until you are tired or the arm begins to ache."

Joel spent days in the pastures with Issachar and the flock. Hamor became somewhat friendlier, and Gaddiel accepted him as if he were just another younger brother. Every day, Joel learned something new about sheep and how to care for them. Issachar had a gentle way with his animals, and he clearly felt tender toward the younger ones. A certain ewe named Nakeh was his favorite. She had a lame back leg that did not keep her from staying with the flock, but sometimes other sheep tried to push her away from the best grass. An old ram butted her, and the other ewes kept their distance. Issachar often gave her special care to make sure she was getting enough food and water and that she would not be injured again. Joel realized there was more to shepherding than he had imagined. In some ways, Issachar had a job like the physician's. The care of the sick and the helpless had been entrusted to them. Their work was honorable.

Many days, Ta-Muit joined the boys. She would leave the house when Joel did, and then she would scamper alongside them on their way through the city, out the gates, and into what Joel had started to call "the best world." When they arrived at pasturage, Ta-Muit scouted the area, and without fail would bring back some prey: mice, voles, frogs, lizards, snakes. She would often eat when Issachar and Joel had their mid-day meal. That was all right so long as Joel didn't have to watch her bite off a head.

These were the happiest times Joel had ever known. As each day went by, he thought less and less about school, and he almost wished his arm would never heal all the way—anything to keep him from having to return to work he hated. He longed to speak with his father about it, but what was the point? Father would never allow him to quit school and become a shepherd.

One evening as they ate, Father told the family he'd finally gone to Grandfather and apologized for his disrespect the day they'd quarreled over Ta-Muit.

"Does he know that the animal is back?" Mother asked.

"I can't say," Father told her.

"You didn't tell him?"

"No, Adah. He didn't ask."

Mother looked amused. "A small point! You should have been honest with him."

"I was! If he had wondered, I would have told him."

"You would have confessed, is what you mean."

Father sighed. "Yes, I suppose so."

"He'll find out that a cat of Egypt now sleeps between your children every night. And when he does—"

"I cannot imagine."

"Will you send Ta-Muit away, then?" Miriam wanted to know. "Because Grandfather will be angry?"

"No, Little Star. I will not send Ta-Muit away."

His sister had raised the question Joel longed to ask. He was glad of the answer, remembering how Father had said this was *his* house, and *he* decided what happened in it.

A day came when Father insisted that Joel see if he could hold a brush and do his work. With heavy heart, he met Benjamin and made his way toward school. Ta-Muit followed along, but she attracted less attention than she once had. People had seen her before, and now she was accepted as a part of the regular morning scene. Children came up and wanted to look at her, then touch her after Joel promised she wouldn't bite or scratch.

They came to the side gate to the temple mount. "Go on, now," Joel told her. "I'll be home later." Ta-Muit looked at him intently, then scampered away. "I wish I were going with you," Joel murmured.

Elishama and the other students welcomed Joel. Being back was not so bad—at first. Everything was familiar, comfortable. He was with friends, especially Benjamin, who whispered, "I missed you."

Elishama told Joel to work for as long as he felt able; if he grew too tired, he could return home. The master was so kind that Joel wanted to please him. He began copying his letters, "to help remember them," Elishama said. Joel wondered how he could ever forget them after making the same marks so many thousands of times.

At first, things went slowly. His right hand felt weak and shaky. Drawing the straight and curved lines was difficult, and Joel felt like a child again. But then his grip became steadier and his copying more accurate. Elishama stopped to see his progress, and he was satisfied.

By mid-morning, though, Joel's arm began to ache. His hand trembled, and his lines wobbled. Soon, he would have to stop. But his thoughts had long ago left the school room. They were with Issachar under the blue sky and white clouds, with the sheep and the grass. Instead of copying letters and words onto papyrus, Joel wished he were drawing in the dust. That had become a regular part of his time in the hills, and each day he could sense that he was becoming more skilled. Maybe he should run away from Jerusalem, find his way to Egypt, and become trained in drawing and painting. But then, there would be no place for him here, in his own home.

Joel worked diligently, but before the mid-day meal, he could do no more. Elishama praised his efforts. He even informed the class that he, Joel, despite his injury, was writing better than most of them. They were lazy good-for-nothings who had no business being in a school when they should be outdoors, working with their muscles and not their empty heads.

Which was exactly what Joel longed to do.

Dismissed, he started home and was not surprised when Ta-Muit appeared from a side street and began walking beside him.

"How do you know where I am and when I'll be there?" Joel asked the cat. "Maybe it *is* true that YAH has sent you."

Only a few people were in the streets. It was mid-day, and people were enjoying their meals indoors. After that, many would rest before resuming the afternoon's work. Joel passed the walls of the royal palace and stopped at the main gate to listen. Maybe he would hear the roars of lions or the cries of birds from the king's private menagerie. Nothing. Then one of the guards, shield in hand and sword strapped to his side, asked what he wanted and told him he had better move along.

But instead of continuing toward home, Joel walked back to the eastern gate of the temple. There were guards here, too, but no one challenged him. "Stay here," he told Ta-Muit. "You can't come inside."

Joel passed through the gate and entered the enormous courtyard before the temple. There were people there, some standing to pray, others consulting with the priests, still others bringing offerings. He wondered if he would see his grandfather; if he did, he could say, truthfully, that he had been dismissed from school and had come to pray.

The temple stood before him. Inside was the Holy Place, and beyond that, the Holy of Holies, where YAH dwelt. So it was said. Joel himself would never see such marvels; only the high priest could enter the Holy of Holies, and that only once a year, on the Day of Atonement.

Joel prayed. His words, when he could form them, made him uneasy: "Let me never return to the school," he pleaded. "YAH, give me a different life."

Surely it was wicked to ask such a thing. But he could not pretend otherwise, certainly not here, where not far from where he stood, YAH sat enthroned above the ark.

He waited to see what would happen, but nothing did. He could find no more words, so he left, feeling as small and helpless as a bird caught in a fowler's snare.

It did help, however, when he found Ta-Muit just where he had left her.

Seventeen

From then on, Joel went to school. Each day his arm ached less and felt stronger. Each day, he stayed longer. Each day, Ta-Muit accompanied him and was waiting for him when he was done. Each day, Elishama was pleased with his work. Each day, his father offered prayers of thankfulness to YAH for his recovery.

Each day, Joel was more and more wretched.

He longed to be in the hills with the sheep. Most evenings now, he spent time at Issachar's house, listening to stories of how the day had gone, how grouchy Hamor was, how the ewe Nakeh was getting along. At last, he confessed to Issachar all his unhappiness.

They were walking through the maze of streets in their part of the city. It was after the evening meal, still light, and they had some time to themselves.

"I hate school!" Joel began. "I can't do it anymore. I want to be a shepherd, like you."

"No, you don't," Issachar corrected him. "It's an awful life. You know that now. You're out in the heat and in the cold. You relieve yourself outside. You smell like your sheep. You're always having to round them up, keep them from falling off a cliff, tend their cuts, and give them medicine. You never know what trouble or danger you're going to face. Listen to me, Joel! You have it good. I'd trade places with you in a moment."

"You'd hate school," Joel objected.

Issachar looked Joel in the eyes. "Tell your father what you're thinking."

"I can't. He'd be angry."

"Why?"

"He'd say I'm ungrateful. Besides, we don't get to change our work, no matter how much we want to."

"Talk to your father," Issachar repeated. "Maybe he'll understand. He's a good man."

Joel couldn't disagree, but the thought still frightened him.

"Promise me," Issachar said.

"All right."

They walked back in silence. At Joel's door, Issachar put a hand on Joel's shoulder. "The blessing of YAH be upon you, my brother."

"And with you," Joel told him.

He'd promised to talk with his father, and he would keep his word. But when—and how—could he find time to do it? It had to be soon, because until then, he would not be able to think of anything else. A hundred times Joel imagined how it would go. Fifty times, Father would understand. He would agree that Joel should leave school and become a shepherd. Fifty other times, Father would accuse Joel of ingratitude. He would express his disappointment. He would shout. Worst of all—in Joel's darkest imagining—he would drag Joel before his grandfather, who would say—things too terrible to contemplate.

The time to talk arrived a day later. Joel was at school. The mid-day meal was past, and the drowsiness of afternoon hung over the classroom. Clearly, he was not the only student who fought to stay awake. He wondered if all the other students would rather be playing outdoors. Sleep had almost overtaken him when Elishama's voice roused him. "Your father is here. You may put away your supplies and go with him. We will see you tomorrow, if YAH wills it."

"Why did you stop for me?" Joel asked, as they began their walk toward home. "It's not time for work to end."

"I had finished my tasks for the day, so I thought we could have time to talk. Your mother and I are worried about you."

"Why?"

"You seem unhappy since you injured your arm. Your expressions betray you. When you believe no one is watching, you look sad. You look as though . . . " Father gazed up at the bright sky.

"As though what, Father?"

"You might be feeling confused about life. About what it means. If that's so, you're not the first boy to feel that way, nor the last. After all, you have thirteen years. You are growing hair in new places. Soon, you will be a man, and you will leave childhood forever. It can be upsetting, even frightening. I am not so old that I've forgotten how I felt. There was a time when I was angry at everything without being able to explain why. Your grandfather and I quarreled every day. He came close to putting me into the street on more than one occasion. It was a terrible time."

Joel had known none of this.

"You can tell me what's inside you," Father went on. "I'll listen and try to understand."

Joel spoke a silent prayer of thanks. He had been wondering how to start a conversation, and his father had done it for him.

"You can tell when I'm not happy?" Joel began.

"As easily as if someone had written the word on a piece of papyrus and hung it around your neck! Never try to lie, Joel. Your face will betray you every time." Father gave his shoulder a gentle squeeze.

"There is something," Joel said. "It's true, Father. I am not happy. I . . . "

Father stopped. The street was empty, and no one would hear. "Yes?" he asked.

"I don't want to be a scribe!"

There. It was out.

"I don't understand," Father said.

"It's what I said. I hate school. I hate spending my days scratching on scraps of papyrus. I don't care about learning how to read or take dictation. I want—a different life."

"You're not making sense! Of course, you want to be a scribe. You always have, ever since I first took you to Elishama. You were excited when he put a brush in your hand and showed you how to copy your letters. You're one of the best students in the class, Joel! Elishama says so. Soon, you'll be finished your studies and come to work with me in the Hall of Scribes. You'll be respected and honored. When the time comes, you'll find a fine wife and give her children, and you will make your mother and me proud grandparents. You will never be in want! How can you say you don't want to be a scribe?"

Joel hung his head. "I know I'm wicked, Papa. Forgive me, but I can't help it."

"Look at me," Father said.

Joel kept his eyes on the dusty street.

"Look at me," Father repeated. This time, he took hold of Joel's chin and raised his head until their eyes met. "You haven't called me 'Papa' in a long time. I had forgotten how it warms my heart."

Tears came to Joel's eyes and he did not try and stop them. "I just can't be a scribe!" he repeated. His voice was loud now. Someone would hear and it would create a scandal. In Jerusalem, families did not display their disagreements in front of their neighbors.

Father put both hands on Joel's shoulders. "I understand. As I said, you're at the door between childhood and manhood. Your feelings are not new, and they're not wrong. But believe me, they will pass, and you'll change your mind. You'll see how blessed you are to be a scribe, and this confusion will leave you."

"It won't! I won't go back to school ever again. I want—"

"What?"

"To be a shepherd like Issachar."

Father looked astonished. "You're joking, but it's not funny."

"I'm serious, Papa! I love being in the hills and helping with the sheep and being with things that are alive! I love the world YAH made, not all this." Joel shrugged his father's hands from his shoulders and spread his arms wide, as if he would embrace all of Jerusalem.

"You are not going to be a shepherd, so you can stop thinking such foolishness right now."

"Papa, please! Understand me!"

Father began to walk again, but he turned into a side street where they were less likely to be overheard.

"I understand that a shepherd's life sounds like a good dream. YAH has created and given us a world of beautiful things. You're not the only boy in Jerusalem who longs for the fields and the hills and the sky. I did, when I was your age. But we cannot all be shepherds."

"It's what I want."

"And I forbid it. Do you intend to end up like Issachar's brothers—always quarreling, dirty, ignorant, drunk with wine all the time?"

"I wouldn't be like that. I would be like Issachar."

"He'll end up like Hamor and Gaddiel," Father predicted. "Half wild and half tame. Like your cat."

"I won't go back to school," Joel declared. "You can't make me."

That was the wrong thing to say. He knew it the moment the words were out.

Father glared at him. "I am trying to be patient with you, Joel, but you will not disrespect my decision for your life. I *can* make you obey me. I've never beaten you, but if that's what it would take—"

"You went against Grandfather!" Joel cried. "You told me he wanted you to be a priest, and you didn't. That's why you became a scribe. Grandfather let you have your way! Why won't you let me?"

Was that another wrong thing to say? Father stopped and looked away. He breathed deeply and slowly. What was he going to do? Joel could feel himself trembling. Never, never in his life had he dared speak to his father this way. It was terrifying, but it made him feel . . . Father had talked about childhood leaving him. He was right. His childhood was gone forever. Now he was a man.

Father turned around. "You are correct about what happened between your grandfather and me. He did allow me to become a scribe. But that happened only after many, many days of bitter fighting. We said things to one another that we remember to this day, and that we wish we had never said. I didn't tell you the whole truth: there *did* come a time when your grandfather put me into the street. Mother begged him to show me mercy, but he would not relent. He said I could return when I was ready to ask forgiveness and obey his will. I said I would never return, and I didn't—not for a long time."

"What did you do?"

"I was too proud to go back and confess I'd been wrong. Father had ordered your aunts and uncles not to take me in, and our neighbors must have heard the same commands. When I was hungry, I begged. I slept in alleys. I thought about running away, of joining the next caravan that came through town. I ended up starved, filthy, cold, and lonely. Father's servant found me and asked me to come home. My absence, he said, was killing my mother. If I didn't return, she would die of a broken heart."

Joel was stunned by his father's story. It was too terrible to be true. But this was no lie. "Did you go back?"

Father nodded. "I threw myself at your grandfather's feet and begged his forgiveness. He raised me up, ordered a bath, and when I was done, had me dressed in clean clothes. My mother could not stop weeping, thanking YAH that her son, who had been dead, was now back alive."

"And Grandfather didn't make you become a priest," Joel said.

"He did not. He told me that he'd found a place for me in Elishama's school and that I could begin my training when I was ready. I went. Your grandfather and I didn't speak of it again, but things were never the same between us. They still are not. It's the great sorrow of my life."

"Grandfather let you have your way," Joel reminded him. "Please let me have mine!"

Certainly, Father would agree. How could he refuse now, after the story he had just shared?

Father and son stood without speaking, their eyes fixed upon one another.

"No," Father said at last. "You are not leaving your school. You are not abandoning your training. You are not going to become a shepherd. These are my wishes, and I expect you to obey me. Soon, you will change your mind and see this foolishness for what it is. We will speak no more about it. Come along. It's time to go home."

Joel was struck speechless. Had he heard correctly? Father was not going to relent? His heart was pounding, and anger unlike anything he had ever felt rose in him and took possession of his words. "I hate you, Papa!" he shouted. "I hate you! I hate school. I hate Jerusalem! I hate my life!"

"I'm certain you do," was all Father said.

Joel dashed down the alley, turned at the corner, and, streaming tears, ran, brushing past startled citizens of Jerusalem, stumbling twice over paving stones, and arriving at home, where he threw open the door, brushed past his mother and sister, made for the ladder, climbed it, threw himself on his sleeping mat, and covered his face with his blanket. Only then did he abandon himself to sobs. When he was exhausted from anger and grief, he fell into welcome sleep.

Eighteen

Joel was wakened by his father's voice telling him it was time to get ready for school. Faint light came through the window, so it was morning. Had he really slept so many hours, missing the evening meal? Why had no one wakened him?

Beside him, Miriam was still dreaming. Ta-Muit was not in her usual place beside her. Perhaps she had already gone outside.

"Joel!" Father called from below. "Come down."

He obeyed. He was thirsty and hungry, and he badly needed to use the latrine. The room below was still in half-darkness; no one had lit an oil lamp. Joel didn't see his mother; she had likely gone up to the Gihon Spring for water. But there was his father, standing in the doorway, facing the street.

Their battle the evening before rose up in Joel again, and he seemed to hear himself shouting, "I hate you! I hate Jerusalem! I hate my life!" Shame filled him as he remembered what had happened. Now he would have to face his father again, for their war was not yet ended.

"Father," he began. "I need the latrine."

The dark silhouette did not move. Father's figure filled the doorway, his back broad and solid, like a wall of stone.

"Father?"

"The blessing of YAH be upon you, my son. It looks to be a fine day."

"Papa?"

Then Father turned and opened his arms. Joel threw himself into them and buried his face in the folds of the tunic.

"I'm sorry, Papa," he whispered. "I didn't mean what I said."

"You said what you felt. I understand, and I forgive you. But my decision has not changed. You will go to school and you will be a scribe. If you can't agree with that, you must find another home. My children will obey me."

Joel's muscles stiffened. Father could tell, and he gathered Joel more closely. Neither spoke. Then, "I love you, son, and I know what's best for you, even better than you know yourself. Do you understand?"

"Yes, Papa," Joel whispered.

"Very well." Father released him. "Get ready for your day. We'll walk together."

Once in the street, Joel looked to see if Ta-Muit had left any prey nearby. Nothing. He went back into the house. "Where's our cat? She's not with Miriam."

"We don't know," Father told him. "She didn't appear last night. Your sister fretted. She's gotten used to having it beside her at night. Miriam says that Ta-Muit helps her to sleep and have good dreams."

Joel was worried. Ta-Muit had become a part of his life—with him in the morning when he awoke, keeping him company on his walks to and from school, even appearing in the pastures to protect him from danger. He remembered what Asher had said: people did not have power over cats; cats were free creatures. They came and went as they pleased, and they offered no explanations.

It was possible, then, that Ta-Muit had found another family. Or had left the city and gone to live among the animals of the field. Perhaps there wasn't enough for her to eat inside Jerusalem.

Such thoughts made him wretched as he used the latrine, washed his face and hands, changed into clean clothes, and ate the morning meal with his family.

When it was time for school, Joel and Father left together, only to be met by Ta-Muit coming toward them, stepping daintily along the street.

"Ta-Muit!" Miriam exclaimed, coming to the door. "I knew you'd come back!"

Mother appeared, and the family gathered around their pet, who, as usual, seemed to love being the center of attention.

Just then, they heard tramping feet and rattling metal. Ta-Muit disappeared inside the house. Here came four soldiers, decked in the insignia of King Solomon's own palace guards. They wore breastplates and helmets of shining metal, and each bore a sword strapped to his side and a dagger in his belt. Their faces looked fierce, their eyes narrow and their jaws clenched.

"What can they want?" Father muttered. "They have no business in this part of the city."

Mother called Miriam to herself. Joel trembled, but he took his stand next to his father.

The guards stopped before them. "Is this the house of Nathan ben-Eliezer?" asked the one who was apparently their leader. He was a massive man, with a chest as broad as a shield and arms as thick as the oak timbers that held up the roof in Joel's house.

"It is," Father replied. "What's the matter?"

"Look!" the leader exclaimed. One of the other guards opened a wicker basket. It was filled with dead birds. "These belonged to His Majesty. The animal that lives here was seen killing them. For that, its life is forfeit."

"It's true that an Egyptian cat often stays here," Father replied, his voice low. "She came to Jerusalem with the last caravan and remained here when the traders went on their way. But it's not possible that she killed the birds. How could she have found her way into the king's palace and then into the place where these lived?"

"That's not mine to answer," the leader declared. "I know only that I have my orders, which are to kill the offender and brings its body to the palace."

"No!" Miriam cried.

"Hush!" Mother told her. "Everything will be all right."

"Indeed," growled the head guard. "Everything *will* be all right when the evil creature is destroyed. Is it here? If so, bring it out and surrender it to me."

Father drew himself up and faced the leader. "What proof have you that the cat destroyed the birds? And how do you know they are the king's?"

"By what right do you question me?" The leader's face was damp with sweat. He kept tugging at his thick black beard. "I come in the name of the king. I ask the questions, and you answer them."

Father was not impressed. "How can you accuse a cat of harming wild birds?"

"They are not wild, I tell you. Sand partridges, they're called. Look at them! Have you ever seen such birds in Israel?"

They did look. The birds were unlike any Joel knew. They were larger than doves, their sides striped brown and white. Each also had a white stripe just above its orange beak, and a white mark that looked like a teardrop on either side of its head.

"Beautiful creatures," Father noted. "I'm sorry they're dead."

"Killed by your cat!" the guard accused.

"I will ask you again," Father told him. "How do you know?"

"The monster was observed inside the palace menagerie, slaughtering the birds! You may be sure that the servants who care for the king's animals keep watch over them day and night. The oil lamps burn always. By their light, a lad saw the cat enter and make its way into their cage, where she did this evil. He tried to capture the beast, but it clawed him and escaped. He will swear on his life that it happened just as he says."

Now Father looked troubled. "Perhaps it is true. Joel, find Ta-Muit and bring her to me."

"No, Papa!" Miriam cried. "The bad men will kill her. See their swords!"

The leader put his hand on the hilt of his weapon, as if he were ready to kill Ta-Muit the moment she appeared.

Joel didn't move.

"Obey me!" Father commanded.

Joel went into the house and looked everywhere for Ta-Muit, but she was gone. The open window in the loft room explained it all. She had escaped.

When Joel reported that Ta-Muit was not inside, the leader ordered his men to enter and search the house. Father blocked their way.

"Move aside," the leader commanded. "In the name of the king."

"I am Nathan ben-Eliezer. My father is one of the most important priests in Israel, second only to the high priest. If you insist on entering my house against my wishes, be sure that he will learn of it and take the matter to Solomon. Free citizens of Jerusalem may not be harassed by such as you."

"I have my orders," the leader answered.

"If my son says the animal is not inside, then she is not. I believe him."

"And why is that?"

"Because he is not a liar."

The leader had no reply to that. But then he recalled his mission. "I must take the cat to the palace, alive or dead."

"But how can you, when the animal is nowhere to be found?"

The man looked puzzled. He kept stroking his beard. "I don't know," he admitted at last.

"We wouldn't want you to face trouble when you go back empty-handed," Father said soothingly. "I pledge you this: when the cat returns, we will bring her to the palace to face the king's justice."

"Papa!" Miriam cried. "No! The mean old king will cut her in pieces!"

Father smiled. "Solomon is neither mean nor old, Little Star. And I doubt that he will cut Ta-Muit in pieces. But if she has destroyed these birds, she must face the consequences."

"She didn't mean it!" Miriam said. "She can't help it."

"Please, Father," Joel added.

Father addressed the soldier. "You have my word that we will bring the cat before the court. That's all I have to tell you today. I hope you'll accept the word of a fellow son of Abraham."

The leader shifted his weight from one hairy leg to the other. He hemmed and hawed, tugged on his beard, and gave in. "Very well. Know this: if you don't keep your word, I will lose my position, and I'll return when you don't expect me. Then we'll settle things, *son of Abraham*."

"I keep my word, *brother*," Father assured him.

"We go," the leader ordered his fellows. With that, they marched away.

Only then did Joel notice that a small crowd had gathered. Nosy neighbors were already whispering among themselves. What else could go wrong?

Nineteen

"INSIDE," Father told the family. He closed the door behind them. "The truth, Joel: is Ta-Muit here?"

"No, sir! I looked everywhere, but she's gone."

"And will not return, if she values her scrawny neck," Father noted. "Adah, do you have a covered basket we can use?"

Mother found one.

"What's it for?" Miriam asked.

"If we find Ta-Muit, we'll put her inside and take her to the king," Father said.

"Don't let him hurt my cat!"

"*My cat*," Joel thought. Then he realized how silly that claim was. What did it matter now *whose* cat Ta-Muit was when her life was in danger? How could she have found her way into the palace? If she'd managed that, how had she done the next thing—kill some of the king's birds?

But how did Ta-Muit accomplish most of the things she did?

"As I told you," Father was saying. "Our king is wise and kind, but justice must be served."

"Ta-Muit didn't mean evil," Joel began. "She was doing what cats do. What YAH created her to do!"

"And how do you know that, since she's the only cat you've ever met?" There was a hint of humor in Father's voice, but it didn't make Joel feel any better.

"It's not fair!" Miriam added.

"Perhaps not," Father agreed. "But the law is the law."

"Then I pray Ta-Muit never comes back," Joel said.

"I don't know if YAH will answer a prayer like that," Father replied. "But I believe He understands your heart. Now it's time for us to go. We're late, but I'll explain to Elishama; you won't be in trouble."

But trouble was waiting for them just outside the door. There was Ta-Muit, perfectly at ease, licking a paw.

"So soon," Father sighed. "Get the basket," he told Joel. "I must deliver this troublemaker to the palace right away. Joel, you'll come with me."

The palace! The thought of going there was frightening, but he was glad to go. He would plead for Ta-Muit's life, even to the king himself.

Ta-Muit did *not* like being imprisoned in the basket, and she immediately voiced her displeasure.

"We'll return as soon as we can," Father promised Mother and Miriam, who was weeping again.

Father and son began their way to the palace. At its gate they were met by six guards who looked like giants. Four carried shields, and the other two stood with drawn swords, ready to defend the royal family.

"Move on," one of the sword guards commanded.

"We have business with the king," Father replied.

"What business?" The guard eyed the basket in Father's hand, from which came the plaintive sounds of Ta-Muit's meowing. "What's in there?" he asked suspiciously. "Let me see."

"A cat," Father replied calmly. "Perhaps you've heard how it killed His Majesty's partridges."

We don't know that for sure! Joel thought.

The guard turned toward his fellows. "There was talk of it yesterday," one said.

"What are our orders?"

"It is to be destroyed," the other replied.

"Please, no!" Joel cried. "YAH sent her to me!"

The head guard stepped back. "How do you know?"

"The boy imagines many things," his father said. "As we all did when we were young."

The guard looked thoughtful. He didn't move—surely a good sign. "Send word to the king's chief counselor," he ordered one of the others.

"We wish to see the king ourselves," Father said.

Joel caught his breath. *Had he heard correctly*? By what right could Father ask to see King Solomon? Joel had seen the king only twice in his life, and that from a long distance, when he was just one in the crowd of people of Jerusalem, all straining their necks to see the king pass in parade at the head of his mighty men, riding in a chariot pulled by Safanad, the mare presented to him by the Queen of Sheba.

The guard chuckled. "So you want to see the king! Who doesn't? Every day people lay siege to the palace gates, begging for His Majesty to hear their complaints and grant them justice for whatever silly causes trouble their silly brains."

"Was it a silly cause when the two women brought a dead child before the king and beseeched him to decide which of them was the babe's true mother?"

Joel felt in awe of his father, who was daring to speak with such boldness here at the gates of the palace.

The guard seemed impressed. "Fair enough," he agreed. "We'll wait to hear what the king's counselor has to say."

They stood in silence, which was broken only by the shrill squalls coming from inside the wicker basket in Father's tight grip.

Before long, the guard returned, and with him came a man dressed in a fine robe, around his neck a chain holding a gold-encircled jewel.

"This is the man, Your Excellency. He claims to have the cat in the basket . . . and he asks to see the king."

The counselor tilted his head and gazed carefully at Joel and his father. "Does he indeed? At least he's telling the truth about having a cat with him. Any fool can hear that."

Joel wondered how the man recognized the sounds Ta-Muit was making, if indeed there had never been cats in Jerusalem before.

"I am Nathan ben-Eliezer," Father said. "Perhaps you know my father."

"All know him," the counselor replied, "and respect him."

Father had made his point. "You are most gracious to speak with us," Father said. "We regret what our cat did to His Majesty's sand partridges, and I'm here to keep my word to the guards sent to my house. Our king is renowned for his wisdom, and we wish to lay our case before him, trusting that he will render a just verdict."

"Who is the lad?" the counselor asked.

"My son, Joel. He studies at the school of Elishama."

"Learning to be a scribe, eh, my boy?"

"Yes, sir."

"And do you work hard?"

"Yes, sir."

"And you like your work?"

What could he say? How could he lie to the counselor, with his father there to hear his words?

"I like it well enough, My Lord." He could not look the counselor in the face, but no "lad," as the man had called him, would dare do that to an elder.

The counselor chuckled. "An honest son," he told Father. "What boy his age likes his work when he could be whiling away his time in games and lazing about, dreaming with his friends about Jerusalem's fair daughters?"

"Indeed," Father agreed. "But this one applies himself. He is one of Elishama's finest students."

"That is good. Work hard, my boy, and a fine career lies before you." The man paused, as if deciding what to do. Then, "Come with me. The king administers justice this morning. He will hear your case if there is time."

The counselor led the way through the courtyard, where palm trees and flowering plants grew in gigantic pots.

They came to the door of the palace, where more guards stood at attention. Then into a hall whose ceiling was held up by slender wooden pillars. Then through a set of bronze double doors thrown open so that Joel could see at the far end a raised platform, richly decorated. Statues of crouching lions lined the aisle leading to a golden throne, and on that throne sat King Solomon himself. Next to him, in crimson robes, her arms encircled with jeweled bracelets, and on her head a slender crown of gold, sat a woman unlike any other that Joel had ever seen. She was not young, but she was like a queen in her bearing. Bathsheba, the king's mother.

Many people crowded the hall. Guards, some priests, scribes sitting cross-legged on cushions, their brushes and ink ready at hand. Joel scanned the crowd, wondering if his grandfather was there. He was not—a relief. Solomon's counselors, richly dressed, stood off to the side of the throne, ready to offer advice should the king request it. And there were people like Joel and Father, ordinary citizens of Jerusalem, who had also come this morning to present their cases.

They waited while Solomon rendered judgments, but Joel and his father were standing so far back in the hall that they could hardly make out what was said. Ta-Muit scratched at the basket, and more than once, Joel had to tell her to hush.

At last, they were called forward. A counselor directed them when to stop, and Joel was face to face with the mighty Solomon, sole ruler of the Kingdom of Israel.

"Kneel before the king," the counselor commanded them. They did. When they were told to stand, Joel dared raise his eyes to the man on the throne. Unlike the other men of the court, Solomon was dressed simply, in a long tunic of finely spun linen. A ring of sapphires was on the fourth finger of his right hand, and a chain of plain gold hung from his neck. His hair was dark and curled, and his brown beard was cut short. He was young, much younger than Joel had expected. He recalled hearing it said that Solomon was only a little older than himself when he took the throne. The king noticed Joel staring at him, and he looked back, directly into

Joel's eyes. Then he raised his left eyebrow, in exactly the way Joel's father did. His expression was curious, serious, but not unkind.

Joel lowered his eyes, but found his gaze pulled toward Queen Bathsheba. Truly, she must be the loveliest woman in the world.

The counselor moved forward to address the court, but the queen gestured to him to wait.

Then she spoke. "And who are these before His Majesty this morning? And what, pray, is in that basket? Something alive, certainly."

True enough, Ta-Muit was meowing wretchedly.

The counselor touched Father's sleeve and gestured that he should speak.

Father told the tale of Ta-Muit from the beginning. Joel kept glancing at the king and his mother, and more than once he saw a faint smile cross their faces.

In a humble but dignified way, Father told the court who he was, a scribe and son of the priest Eliezer, who had rendered service to the temple since it was built, more than ten years ago. He defended Ta-Muit's actions, noting what a skilled rat catcher she was, and how much enjoyment she had brought not only to their family, but to the children living on their street.

"What he does not mention, however," broke in the counselor, "is that this creature found its way into Your Majesty's menagerie and destroyed many of your precious sand partridges." He clapped his hands, and a servant came forward with the basket of dead birds. "Life for life," he continued. "All in Jerusalem know that it is death to steal from the king."

Solomon had been listening attentively to this speech, but he could not take his eyes off the basket in Father's hand.

The counselor finished, and all was silent. Joel's heart was thumping so strongly that he wondered if everyone in the room could hear it.

The king glanced at his mother, and she gestured toward Ta-Muit's basket. He understood her intention.

"Let's see this fearsome creature, slayer of my property."

A servant came forward to take the basket from Father.

"No!" cried the counselor. "It may be a dangerous animal, a cobra, perhaps, brought into the king's presence through cunning, taught to bite and kill anyone who disturbs it."

"There is no cobra in the basket, is there, scribe?" the king asked Father.

"No, Sire. Only the cat, Ta-Muit, as we told you."

"So the animal has a name?" The king sounded amused. "Very few animals I know of have names."

"The boy from Egypt told me her name," Joel explained. Immediately he knew he'd made a mistake. No one spoke in the presence of the king without being asked.

The king did not seem offended. "Ta-Muit," he replied. "I wonder if it has a meaning?"

"Killer of the king's birds," ventured the counselor.

The king gave him a look. "I doubt that," he replied.

"Your majesty knows best," the counselor said, lowering his eyes.

"More likely the name means 'Maker of Mischief.' Would that be correct, scribe?"

"It would seem so," Father agreed. "She has caused us much trouble."

"Let us see this mischief maker," the king said. He gestured to Father to approach the throne. Two guards, swords at the ready, advanced as well.

"The cat has a cord around her throat, to restrain her," Father explained. He, too, had spoken without being addressed.

"I can't imagine she appreciates that," Solomon answered.

"No, Your Majesty."

"Open the basket."

Father placed the basket onto the polished stone floor. Cautiously, Father undid the lid. "Come here," he told Joel.

Joel looked at the king, waiting for permission. The king nodded.

Joel knelt by the basket and spoke soothing words to the cat. "Quiet, now," he whispered. "No mischief."

Father opened the lid slowly. Sure enough, Ta-Muit made as if to jump out, but quicker still, Joel grabbed the cord and held tight. When she knew she could not escape, the cat allowed Joel to lift her from the basket and hold her close to his chest. He stood and faced the king.

"This is Ta-Muit, Your Majesty."

Then the king surprised him. He got up from his throne, came down the steps and advanced toward him.

Ta-Muit growled.

Twenty

"Ha!" the King exclaimed. "A fierce beast, indeed! You dare show your teeth to your king!" Then he laughed, and everyone in the room laughed with him.

The king held out his hands toward Joel. "May I?" he asked.

"I don't want her to scratch or bite Your Majesty," Joel replied.

"Don't worry. I've handled beasts far larger." He took Ta-Muit from Joel's hands. The cat growled again, but the king began stroking her behind the ears and spoke quietly to her—in Egyptian!

How did the king know that cats love to have their heads scratched, and how did he know Egyptian?

King Solomon continued to stroke Ta-Muit, who relaxed in his grasp. "You are wondering how I know the ways of cats," he said to Joel.

"Yes, Your Majesty. And—"

"And what? Speak up, lad."

"And how you know Egyptian."

The king smiled. "My wife, the lady Isetnofret, is daughter to Pharaoh. A wise husband does well to learn his wife's native language so that she cannot speak ill of him without his understanding what she is saying."

The courtiers laughed again.

Solomon started walking around the hall, always stroking Ta-Muit and speaking softly. He had a natural way with her, and Joel remembered how it was said YAH had blessed the king with special knowledge of animals and their ways.

"And you are wondering how I know of cats. I will tell you. All know there are no cats in Jerusalem—not now, that is. But once –" the king looked toward his mother— "once there was another cat in Jerusalem. *My* cat. A gift from the Queen Bathsheba. Isn't that so, Mother?"

"Yes. You were only a small boy. Merchants from Tyre came to trade with your father, David. They brought a cat, just as the Egyptian traders have done. Your father took you with him while he spoke with the men from that great city by the sea, for he wanted you to learn from the beginning the work of royal princes. When you returned to the palace that day, you had the cat with you. My Lord, King David, explained that the Tyrian cat seemed to have cast a spell over you, and how the traders, wishing to please My Lord, made it a gift."

"I remember," the king said sadly. "Azmelqart."

The king continued to stroke Ta-Muit. "He looked much like this one. Tawny, dark stripes, the white chin. But larger than this one, who is, I supposed, a female?"

"Yes, My Lord," Father said.

The king felt Ta-Muit's sides. "And soon to be a mother, unless I mistake myself."

"Kittens?" Joel exclaimed before he could stop himself. "How?"

"The usual way, I suppose," Solomon replied. Again, people laughed.

"But she's the only cat in Jerusalem," Joel replied.

"Then she was expecting before she arrived. Before long, there will be more than one cat in our city." The king was silent, and his thoughts seemed to be far away. "I loved that renegade Azmelqart," Solomon went on. "He obeyed no laws but his own, and so he was always getting himself into scrapes."

"He was your constant companion," Queen Bathsheba remembered. "He would follow the king everywhere," she said to the court. "Slept on his bed. Drank from his own bowl. And . . . "

The queen's voice faded out, and she chuckled. "And ate from his own dish at the king's own table!"

"My father didn't approve," King Solomon assured everyone. "I was permitted to share my table with Azmelqart only when King David was not at home."

"My son speaks truly," Queen Bathsheba added. "A cat, we soon learned, is not yours to command, even if you are a prince of Israel. Rather, a cat permits you to sit at table with *him*. King David allowed no one to tell him what to do, so rather than lose to a cat from Tyre, he would absent himself. Who won that battle?"

"Azmelqart, Mother," King Solomon replied. He looked at Joel and Father. "I dare say you have had a similar experience with this one?"

"Yes, My Lord. She knows her own mind and how to get her way."

"So did Azmelqart. Perhaps he was too independent. He would not be confined to the palace, and one night, he dragged himself into my bed chamber, torn and bleeding. Wild dogs, we surmised. He came to my arms and there he died."

All was hushed in the hall.

The king roused himself. "My father saw how deeply the death of Azmelqart hurt me, and he ordered that no more cats should be permitted in Jerusalem. He feared that if I were to possess another—and lose it—the pain would be too great." Solomon paused, thinking. "I wonder now if he was right."

"Royal decrees cannot be wrong, My Lord," the counselor reminded him.

The king came to Joel. "Will your cat behave herself if the king so decrees?"

How could he answer such a question? Joel felt all eyes on him. "Yes, My Lord."

"Ask her." He handed Ta-Muit back to Joel.

"Obey your king," Joel whispered. Ta-Muit purred contentedly, then she put a paw up to his face.

Solomon chuckled. "You have the gift, Joel ben-Nathan. You *do* speak the language of animals."

"How can you tell, My Lord?"

The king looked at him kindly. "I just know. Come with me—and bring the offender." He gave Ta-Muit a quick pat on the head. "Wait here," he told the assemblage. "We shall return shortly."

"My Lord, do you not want someone to accompany you?" began the counselor.

The king held up a hand. "That won't be necessary. I want only the lad and his cat."

The man nodded in submission.

"Come," the king told Joel.

Joel looked at his father, who nodded that he should go.

Solomon made his way to the open door on the right side of the hall. People bowed as he passed. Again, Joel felt all eyes on him, and he could only wonder what the courtiers thought about someone like himself being asked further into the royal palace.

The king led the way down a hall whose walls and floor were polished stone. They came to a pillared courtyard whose four sides were covered but whose middle was open to the sky. The central square was green with plants in pots, many more than Joel had seen before. Palm trees, bushes covered with flowers, vines hanging from arbors of iron. In the center of the courtyard stood a fountain, where stone fish spouted water from their gaping mouths. The basin in which it sat was planted with papyrus, and through the surface of the pool grew lotus and lilies among flat green leaves as large as serving platters.

Bird cages hung from metal standards, themselves shaped to resemble trees with twisting branches. A constant chatter arose from all sides. In cages along the walls Joel saw animals he did not know. He recognized monkeys like the one the Egyptian trader had with him, but others, some with faces that looked painted with colorful stripes and others whose bottom ends were bright pink, were beyond anything he could imagine. The king led the way slowly around the courtyard, stopping when he came to an enormous cage that held a pair of spotted cats many times the size of Ta-Muit. They were not lions, and Joel guessed that they were cheetahs. Ta-Muit's muscles tensed, and Joel feared the cat would wriggle from his arms and dash from the room.

King Solomon noticed. “Make her remember her promise,” he said.

Joel spoke softly to the cat.

“Put her down,” the king told him.

This was risky, but Joel had to obey. He set Ta-Muit on the floor. One of the cheetahs growled at her and showed its fangs. The cat, for her part, made a threatening noise in her own throat. The hair on her back bristled up, and she arched her back. But Ta-Muit stood her ground. The cheetah sat, its forepaws extended in front of it. The cat approached the cage, and the cheetah leaned forward toward the bars. Then the two animals touched noses.

Twenty-one

King Solomon laughed out loud. "The little one will not be easily frightened. She has courage, an important virtue in animals and men."

"My Lord?"

Joel glanced around, looking to see who had spoken. He had thought he and the king were the only ones in the courtyard.

Coming toward them was a young woman of such extraordinary beauty that Joel wondered if she were a vision. She was young, perhaps only a couple of years older than himself. Her skin was pale, paler than that of Israelite women. She was slender and delicate, like a papyrus reed. Like the king, she was dressed simply, in a long white tunic of shimmering fabric lighter than linen. Around her neck, a beaded necklace with a scarab of lapis lazuli at its center, and on her head, a wig of elaborately braided black hair. Her eyes were circled in black, too. Her expression was sad.

Two girls, also dressed in the Egyptian style, followed behind her and took their places on either side of the door through which the young woman had come.

Joel knew that King Solomon had married the daughter of Pharaoh, so this must be—his queen, the Egyptian Queen of Israel. Without thinking, he dropped to one knee.

"My Lady, this is Joel ben-Nathan, possessor of Jerusalem's only cat."

The Queen advanced, and her husband extended his hand. She took it and held it briefly to her lips. Solomon nodded to acknowledge her.

"You may rise, Joel ben-Nathan," the king told him. "This is my queen, Isetnofret."

"Your Majesty," he whispered hoarsely. He felt foolish and ugly, unfit to be in a place of such unearthly beauty, with a son and a daughter of mighty kings. Not knowing anything else to do, he simply stood.

Ta-Muit knew what to do. She left Joel's side and approached the queen, who smiled and dropped to her knees before the cat.

"Cats rule us all," Solomon noted. "Perhaps it's a good thing there have been no cats in Israel these many years! None to challenge my right to the throne."

The queen could not stop petting Ta-Muit. Her happiness was obvious. Although she was gorgeously dressed, the queen could have been any girl taking delight in a living creature. Joel wished that Miriam were there to see this moment. He felt sure that Queen Isetnofret would be kind to her.

Solomon spoke to his wife at some length, but it was in Egyptian. She replied, and her voice was sweet, but wistful.

"She doesn't yet speak or understand much of our language," the king explained. "She asked where your cat came from, and I told her from Egypt. That made her homesick. My lady greatly misses her family. She has slave girls as companions, but they don't take the place of her mother and sisters. She is devoted to her father and sends word to him often. I try to make her happy—" the king opened his arms to take in the courtyard and its rich life—"but . . . "

Joel didn't know what to say. How could anyone be unhappy in this place?

"People may think that being born into royalty assures a fine life—a happy life," the king continued. "But it's hard. The queen didn't choose me for husband. She was sent to me by her father to forge an alliance between our two nations. Nor did I choose her.

My counselors arranged it all. She will never admit it, but I think she wishes she were not here, not married to a king. To . . . me."

Joel could hardly believe that Solomon would reveal such secrets to him, a mere nobody. The king walked into the open courtyard, and Joel followed even though he had not been invited. Where did such foolish presumption come from? He did not know. Meanwhile, Queen Isetnofret was enjoying playing with Ta-Muit, paying no mind to the king and Joel at all.

The king stopped by the fountain and extended a hand into a fine spray of water shooting from the mouth of a wide-eyed fish. He wiped the hand on his face and beard.

Then he realized that Joel had followed him. He turned, and in his face Joel saw the same sorrow that marked the youthful features of the Egyptian queen.

"May I tell you a secret, Joel ben-Nathan?"

"If Your Majesty wishes it."

"And will you keep it?"

"I swear by my life."

"Oh, not by something so precious as that," the king told him. "In fact, don't swear at all. I take you at your word."

"Thank you, My Lord."

"I became king when I wasn't many years older than you. I had fewer than twenty years. How many have you?"

"Thirteen, Your Majesty."

"Almost old enough to become a king!"

"I don't know—"

"Here is my secret. I didn't want the throne. Others wanted it for me. My brother, Adonijah, desired it for himself, and I would have let him have it, except that—"

The king stopped, as if he were about to say too much.

"Except that others made sure he did not obtain it. I was crowned king. I have done my duty to YAH and to my father, David, and to my people. But sometimes I wish . . . "

The king lapsed into silence; the sorrow came over him again.

"My Lord?"

"That I had a different life. Just as she—" he nodded to where Isetnofret was playing with Ta-Muit—"wishes she were back in Egypt with her family, whom she loves so much—more than she loves me."

Joel was struck dumb by what he had heard. It couldn't be true, what the king said. It wasn't right that he had opened his mind so fully to a person such as himself. He needed to leave this place, pretend he'd heard none of the king's confession. It was not fitting.

"Forgive me," Solomon told him, as if he had read his thoughts.

"There is nothing to forgive. You are the king."

Solomon sighed. "For better or worse. Tell me, Joel, how is it with you? Are you happy with the life YAH has laid before you?"

What could he say? Confessing to Father had been hard, the hardest thing he had ever done, and look how it had turned out. He wanted to turn and run from the palace, through the city gates and into the pastures where he and Issachar could talk and laugh and drink warm milk together. But that could not be.

"You don't answer," the king told him, "but your silence tells me that you are not happy. I am right, am I not?"

"Your Majesty sees everything," Joel replied.

Solomon laughed. "Come now! You are not one of my courtiers. They say such silly things because they feel they must. I thank YAH I do *not* see everything, or know everything, or understand everything. But I am right about you. Tell me of your unhappiness."

Joel did, beginning with hearing the birds winging over Jerusalem and longing to join them on their journeys. He told of the Egyptian traders, and Seb, and meeting Ta-Muit. Of the cat's finding his house and bringing gifts of slain rats and mice. Of causing him to fall from the ladder and break his arm. How he was given permission to join Issachar in the hills with the sheep, and how Ta-Muit had killed the asp to protect him. And of how he had come to hate school and the thought of spending his life as a scribe, even though that was his father's decree.

The king listened to every word. "What would you like to be, Joel ben-Nathan, if you had your way?"

Joel couldn't look his king in the eye. "A shepherd," he whispered. "To live in the hills, with the animals. To see the birds in flight, the lizards, foxes, even the locusts and ants. I know I'm ungrateful. Being a scribe is a noble calling. And being a shepherd is . . . "

"Is what?" Solomon asked.

"Is to become a wild man, Father says."

The king chuckled. "Perhaps your father is right. You surely have heard that *my* father was a shepherd in his youth, and he was indeed a wild man all his life, until his sad end."

How could Joel have forgotten the stories of David, slayer of lion and bear? Who left his sheep to kill the giant and find favor in the court of Saul, and later to become king himself?

"There's nothing dishonorable about being a shepherd," Solomon told him. "But your father is right: being a scribe is a great privilege. You'll win respect and earn high wages. And you will possess the secrets of writing and reading, secrets I myself do not possess."

Once again, Joel wondered if had heard right. What was the king telling him?

"You Majesty doesn't know how to write or read?" He realized how insolent the question must sound to the wise Solomon.

The king was not offended. "No, lad. I don't know how. I have no need, not with men like your father to copy my every word and to read to me anything I request. If you finish your studies at Elishama's school, there might well be work for you in my court, listening and writing down my words. Some of them are reported to be wise. Perhaps they are."

"Your Majesty is kind to have listened to my story. I am only . . . " Joel could find no words, but he had to do something to show the king his thanks. He dropped to one knee and bowed his head.

The king raised him up. "What are we to do with you, Joel ben-Nathan? You are unhappy, but you must obey your father's wishes. I will not repay his faithful service by taking his authority from him."

"My Lord."

The king put a hand on his shoulder. "I thank you for speaking honestly. And for sharing your wisdom."

"I am not wise," Joel told him. "I don't understand many things."

"Nor do I, but you understand something many people never do: your own spirit. To know yourself—that is the beginning of wisdom."

Twenty-two

Just then, the counselor came into the courtyard. "Forgive me, Majesty, but people are wondering why you and the lad are gone so long. You have more cases to judge, and some people are becoming impatient."

"Let them wait!" Solomon thundered. "I am their king! They will wait all day if I wish it."

He winked at Joel. "Go now and tell them the king answers to no one's impatience. You are forgiven for interrupting our conversation."

"Your Majesty," the counselor said. Then he hurried from the room.

When he was gone, the king laughed. "A good man, but he's learned his role too thoroughly. He's right, though. It's time for us to return to the court."

They went to the queen, who had become fast friends with Ta-Muit in the short time they had been together. She stood in the presence of her husband, and the cat came to Joel. Solomon spoke to her, and she responded sadly.

"I told her that we must go. My Lady wishes me to thank you for bringing your cat to meet her."

Then Joel knew what he wanted to do. He picked up Ta-Muit and put her into the arms of the queen. "She is for you," he told her. "I want you to have her."

It was the most difficult thing he had ever done. Ta-Muit had come to *him*, but the queen needed her much more than he did.

His world was here, but the queen had no one. The king was surely kind to her, but she longed for her own family, her own country.

Solomon explained what Joel was offering. Tears came to the queen's eyes, but she blinked them back.

She spoke in broken words to Solomon. "My Lady thanks you for such a noble gift," he told Joel. "She wants you to know it's the most precious thing anyone has ever offered her."

"Thank you, My Lady," Joel said. He could feel tears in his eyes, too, but he would not cry in front of his king.

"However," Solomon went on, "the queen cannot accept your gift. She says that the gods of her country brought the cat to *you*, and you are meant to keep her."

Isetnofret gestured for Joel to take his cat. He did, feeling overwhelmed by all that had happened, all that he had learned in the moments since following the king into the courtyard.

The queen nodded to Joel, spoke a brief word to the king, then glided away.

The king looked at him, and Joel saw more than kindness in his eyes. He saw respect. It was too much for him, and he turned away.

"You have a generous spirit, Joel," the king told him. "That is more precious than all the wisdom of the world. Come, now. We've kept the court waiting long enough."

Ta-Muit held tightly in his arms, Joel followed the king back to the hall of judgment. Solomon took his throne, acknowledged his mother, and gestured to Joel to stand before him.

"Hear this, all people of Jerusalem: by my decree, the cat known as Ta-Muit is found guilty of destroying a goodly number of sand partridges."

Joel tensed.

"But she is hereby pardoned for her crime. No one may exact punishment or retribution against her or the family of Nathan ben-Eliezer, on penalty of my displeasure."

Even as the king spoke, his scribes were busily writing down his words.

"The price of her pardon is two of her kittens when they are born. I wish to make them a gift to My Lady, Queen Isetnofret."

The king left his throne and stood facing Joel. The room went silent; kings did not leave their thrones to speak with their subjects. To Ta-Muit he whispered, "Try to be good, for your own sake. We don't want to lose you." Then, in a loud voice, he continued: "Know further that should this cat again trespass in the royal palace or harm anything in it, then her life is forfeit." With a low voice, he said to the cat, "I know you understand me. For the sake of the lives within you, obey. And obey this young man who is your master. Now you may go," he told Joel. "I have other judgments to make this day, but I don't think I shall have another like this one."

Holding Ta-Muit close, Joel took a few steps backwards, then turned to leave the hall. His father joined him. On either side, people looked at them with curiosity.

Outside, the sun was blinding and the air much hotter than in the shaded rooms of the palace. They put Ta-Muit into the basket, and Joel told her to remember what the king had said, how she must behave from now on. He let out a deep breath, and then his tears came. He knew he should be filled with joy, and he was. But mostly he felt stunned, unable to take in all that he had just seen and heard, all that the king had shared, and then his merciful decree. And he felt the weight of his new responsibility: it was up to him, no one else, to make sure that Ta-Muit stayed and was kept safe until her babies were born. He wanted nothing better than to bring two of them to the queen, in hope that they would ease her longing for her own land.

Outside the palace gate, Father stopped and gave Joel a searching look. "Can you tell me what occurred while we were left in suspense, waiting for you to return?" he asked. "Or is it a secret?"

"It's not a secret," Joel replied, but he felt reluctant to share everything that had passed between himself and the king, especially about how unhappy he was being a scribe. He shared most of the rest, though—how he met the queen, and how sad she seemed, and how King Solomon had revealed her homesickness. He told how the queen was delighted with Ta-Muit, and how he had offered her the cat as a gift.

"You were going to give Ta-Muit to a stranger?"

"She's not a stranger! We talked some—the king translated for us—and I found out how much she misses her family. I thought having Ta-Muit could help her feel happier."

"Even though you believe YAH sent her to you."

Joel couldn't recall saying that to his father in so many words, but it was the truth. "Yes, sir," he confessed.

"It must have been difficult to offer your cat," Father told him.

"Yes, sir."

"And the queen did not accept it."

"No."

"YAH bless you, Joel. You have proven yourself a man today. Now I must go to my work. Take Ta-Muit home, and if you feel strong enough, go to school. Elishama will wonder where you are."

Twenty-three

Two unusual events occurred that evening. First, while the family was eating their meal, a servant from the king's palace appeared with a dish of food for Ta-Muit. "His Majesty wants you to know that portions from his own table will be brought to you every day until the cat known as Ta-Muit is delivered of kittens and they are weaned. She should not have to hunt for her food among unclean animals such as rats and mice."

"Tell the king we humbly thank him," Father said. "He is generous."

"He is," the servant agreed. "I will deliver your message, Nathan ben-Eliezer."

Joel uncovered Ta-Muit's meal, a portion of roasted lamb. It smelled delicious; he himself had not enjoyed meat for many days.

Ta-Muit would be eating richer food than any of the rest of them—food from King Solomon's own table.

It was almost enough to make him jealous of his pet.

For her part, Ta-Muit devoured the meat and retired to a bed Miriam had devised for her, where she spent a long time licking herself, with special attention to her paws. Then she fell asleep.

The second event occurred just as Ta-Muit was settled. Grandfather appeared at the door and stomped into the house without being invited. His dark brows were knit and his mouth was set in a grim line.

"Welcome!" said Father. "Why didn't you let us know you wanted to visit? Adah would have been glad to prepare you a meal."

"Welcome, Father-in-Law," Mother added. "I have some stew and am glad to warm it for you."

"I didn't come to eat," Grandfather grumbled. "I came to find out just what is going on in this household."

Father gestured toward a bench. "Please, sit and tell us what you mean."

Just then, Grandfather noticed Ta-Muit, who had awakened and was watching him with narrowed eyes. The hair on her back was raised a bit, too.

"Why is that cat in the house?" the old man demanded. "Why does it still live, after killing the king's partridges?"

"You've heard about that, then," Father said.

"All of Jerusalem has heard. Wild stories are everywhere. I want the truth!"

"Joel will tell you, but let's remain calm. There's no need for upset."

Grandfather took in a deep breath and blew it out. "Very well," he agreed. "But I want to hear it from you, not the boy."

"Joel is no longer a boy," Father replied. "And because I wasn't invited into the king's private rooms, I can't tell you exactly what was said. Only your grandson can do that. I promise he will tell the truth. Joel, please tell your grandfather what happened in the palace."

Joel recounted that one of the keepers in Solomon's menagerie had seen Ta-Muit killing the sand partridges and how the guards had brought them to the house, demanding that the cat be delivered up to justice. Grandfather kept glaring at Ta-Muit, who gazed back at him.

"That much everyone knows," Grandfather said. "I want to hear what happened when the king took you into his garden."

"He wanted to show me his animals," Joel explained. "He said I have a gift for understanding them and their language."

"Bah! YAH has given us dominion over the beasts of the field and the birds of the air, but they cannot speak *with* us. Nevertheless, our king is full of such fanciful thoughts. What else happened, besides His Majesty showing you his menagerie?"

"The queen came into the garden, and she played with Ta-Muit. The king says she misses her family and the cat made her feel less lonely."

"Rubbish! Why would the king speak of such things to someone like you?"

"I'm telling the truth," Joel insisted. "I saw how much the queen enjoyed Ta-Muit, and I offered to give her my cat as a gift."

"That, at least, was sensible. Why didn't she accept?"

"I don't know, Grandfather. But the king told the court that when Ta-Muit has her kittens, he wants two of them for himself. He'll give them to the queen."

"He would do much more for that woman!" Grandfather exclaimed. "He allows her to worship her idols in his own palace. He builds shrines for them. Some say that he secretly prays to them himself. Abomination! I wish he had never married that girl, but his counselors insisted. 'An alliance with Egypt is a good thing,' they kept saying. 'What better way to seal it than through the joining of two royal houses?' Have they gone mad? Have they forgotten what the Egyptians did to our ancestors, and now we bring their gods into Jerusalem?"

Grandfather's voice was getting louder and louder.

"We promised to stay calm," Father reminded him.

"It is said that he loves the girl, but she does not return his feelings. He'll do anything to please her. If he cannot, she will tell her father, and Pharaoh will be avenged."

"Then why didn't he seize Ta-Muit today?" Father asked. "He could have taken the cat without Joel's permission. Instead, even after Joel offered her as a gift, he and the queen refused."

"They will take her young," Grandfather retorted. "And they may change their minds. If the Egyptian girl desires a plaything, the guards will be here again, and this time, the animal will be gone for good."

Which would please you, Joel thought. "You're wrong," he said. "The king is kind. He wouldn't take her after refusing my offer." Right away, he knew he'd been too bold. Grandfather believed himself always in the right, and he would allow no contradiction, especially from one he regarded as still a child.

Grandfather ignored this insulting backtalk. "The king will do as he wishes, even build temples to idols to gratify his wives, and no one can stop him. But YAH sees—and judges."

He pushed himself to his feet. "Don't let your interview with the king turn your head," he warned Joel. "Just because he brought you to his garden, don't conclude you are anyone exceptional."

"There's no need—" Father began.

"I am leaving," Grandfather interrupted. He looked at Ta-Muit again. "The sooner this creature is gone, the better it will be for you all. Deviltry! It has no place in Israel, not here, and not in the palace, no matter if this latest consort of the king *is* a pretty plaything from Egypt."

With that, he left.

The family sat in silence until Father spoke. "Don't take his words to heart," he advised Joel. "He's old and set in his ways, and he worries. But if the king's love has led him to build shrines for the gods of Egypt, then I agree: that should not be."

Lying on his sleeping mat that night, Ta-Muit curled between himself and Miriam, Joel thought about his grandfather's words. Did King Solomon dare allow shrines to the idols of Egypt in Jerusalem itself? That could not be right. Then he thought of Queen Isetnofret and how beautiful she was. He could still see her slender form and the way her tunic shimmered in the sunlight. Joel had never yet thought much about girls, even though he understood that one day, he would marry and become the father of children. In a few years, his parents would seek a suitable bride for him; they and her parents would make the arrangements for the girl and Joel to meet. Then the matter would be settled, and Joel would have a wife.

He knew about the ways of husbands and wives together, and he had heard the talk of some older boys about things his father would say he was still too young to know. He remembered how Issachar had once held a mirror from Egypt, its handle the form of a lovely goddess not wearing any clothing at all.

And Joel could not help but think about Isetnofret and King Solomon. She was hardly older than Joel, but she was a married woman, and the king a strong young warrior. Perhaps one day soon, the queen would bear a child . . .

He thought back to the splendor of the king's palace, its courtyard garden, and the wonderful creatures that lived there for His Majesty's pleasure. Joel's own home was small, uninteresting, shabby by comparison. His arm was healing rapidly, and even tomorrow he had to return to school. One day, he would complete his training and take up the tasks YAH and his father had assigned him. It seemed as if Joel could see his life stretching before him, an endless drudgery. He would have a wife to care for, and children, and work to earn money so they would not starve. Somewhere this night, Seb was sleeping under the stars, strange sights and languages and ways of doing things all around him. In the royal palace, King Solomon might this very moment be embracing his Egyptian queen or one of his other wives, doing his duty to raise up sons, one of whom would one day take his seat on Israel's throne.

And here he was—just Joel.

Twenty-four

The days passed, one much like another. Joel's arm healed so well that he no longer needed it splinted. He was at school full days again, days that seemed unending. Every morning he wished he could go to the pastures with Issachar. Every day, Ta-Muit grew a bit more plump, fattened by the rich foods that came from the palace and by the kittens growing inside her. Soon, she would be a mother, and when the kittens were weaned, Joel would let the king have his choices.

Ta-Muit must have understood Solomon's warnings, for now she did not wander from the house. She had a knack of always finding sunny places for napping, and Miriam took to mothering her in a sickeningly sweet way that set Joel's teeth on edge. But Ta-Muit put up with it.

As the days went by, they grew warmer and warmer. The dry season was approaching, and soon there would be no rain at all. But one morning, the sky was thick with heavy clouds. The air did not move, and pesky flies made their way into the house, annoying Mother by trying to get a taste of the morning meal. Miriam complained of fever, and Mother said that yes, she was ill and must stay on her sleeping mat.

Issachar appeared at his usual time. "Storms on the way," he predicted. "It won't be a good day to tend sheep."

"You'll get soaked," Joel told him. "And the sheep, too."

"I don't worry about the animals," Issachar replied. "Their wool is so thick that water rolls right off it. I have my shepherd's cloak, so I'll be all right."

"Be careful," Mother said. "If a storm comes near you, find shelter."

"There's a hut where we can huddle in bad weather. And look here." He took a small object from his pouch. Joel recognized it immediately: an amulet. "All us shepherds have them. They protect us from dangers, including storms."

"May YAH himself bless and keep you," Mother said.

"And you and your family," Issachar told her.

He went his way, leading Laban, Dodo, and his other charges. As usual, Joel longed to go with them, but this day might be one more safely spent in the city.

School was more difficult than usual because so little light came through the windows. Even the older boys, who always had first choice of where to sit, were grouchy and complained about how they couldn't see to work. Finally, in the afternoon, Elishama told them to pack up their tools and go home.

By now, the sky was the color of slate. The air had begun to stir, and swirls of dust played in the streets as Joel and Benjamin made their way home.

Mother met them and said that Miriam was very sick with fever. She sent Joel for the physician, who came immediately. He climbed into the loft, followed by Mother and Joel. They found Miriam sleeping fitfully, her forehead drenched with sweat. Her clothes were damp, as well. The faithful Ta-Muit was by her side, and she did not move even while the physician examined the girl and told Mother what to do.

He produced a small clay vial and woke Miriam so that she could drink from it. "This will help," he promised. "You must be sure she drinks much water, as much as you can get her to swallow."

"Joel, go to Gihon Spring right now and fill two jars," Mother instructed him.

He went down the ladder, careful of his footing. A jar in each hand, he made his way up the hill. The air was moving faster now, and off in the distance he could hear thunder. It had been a hot day, but now it had grown chilly.

When he returned with the water, the physician was just leaving. "Your sister will recover. I have left medicine with your mother and have placed a healing amulet in a pouch around her neck. She needs cool water on her face and arms to help break the fever. Assure your mother that the girl will be all right. Mothers worry about their children." He patted Joel's shoulder. "And your arm, it's all better now?"

Joel assured him that it was, and the physician went his way. "Your father may send you later with my payment, but don't worry about it this evening. We are about to have a great storm."

In the loft, Mother was tending Miriam, who had fallen into a calm sleep. Joel brought water cool from the spring and pieces of cloth for his sister's forehead and arms.

"Will you take care of her while I prepare the meal?" Mother asked him. "She's sleeping deeply, so there shouldn't be much to do. And ask YAH to heal her, as I've been doing."

Joel promised. He sat beside Miriam, praying for her recovery. Ta-Muit roused and settled in his lap. She began to purr; Miriam, roused, found her head and patted it.

By the time Father arrived, the rain had begun. "The streets are turning to mud," he told them. "And I am wet down to my skin."

Mother found him some dry clothes. He wanted to know how Miriam was, and Joel was able to call down from the loft that she was sleeping and that her fever was less. Father came up and told Joel he could help Mother prepare the meal. He himself would stay with Miriam and pray for her without ceasing.

Ta-Muit made as if to follow Joel down the ladder. She had been able to manage it on her own until just a few days ago, but her bulging belly made her less sure-footed than usual. Joel gathered her into his arms and came down.

"You're heavy," he told her. "When are you going to have these kittens?"

The cat made for the door and began scratching it frantically.

"You can't go outside," Joel told her. "Not in this storm." In fact, the wind was stronger than ever, the rain pelted down, and the darkness outside was being shattered by strikes of lightning. But Ta-Muit kept pawing at the door, meowing in distress.

"Let her out," Mother advised. "If she doesn't like it, she'll come back."

"How will I tell? I couldn't hear her above the storm."

"Then watch by the door until she does return. I don't think it will be long."

When Joel opened the door, Ta-Muit ran out. Right away, she was hidden in the dark and rain.

"Let her come back," Joel prayed.

His prayer was answered, for not long afterward, he could hear the sound of pitiful mewing outside, and the faint noise of Ta-Muit's claws on the door. He let her in, and her appearance was so strange and comical that he had to keep from laughing. The cat was drenched, and all her fur was plastered down against her body. Only then did Joel realize that Ta-Muit's body was smaller than he imagined it to be. Beneath her glorious spotted and striped coat, she was lean, all except for her bulging belly.

"Get a cloth and dry her," Mother advised. "The poor thing is soaked."

Joel did. Then she shook herself and made her way to the bed Miriam had devised, where she began the slow and precise process of giving herself a tongue bath.

Father came down the ladder. "Miriam is resting well. Her fever is breaking. She will be fine."

"Thanks be to YAH," Mother said. "Fever is serious. My mother died of it."

Father was quick to comfort her. "Our Little Star will rest well, and in the morning, she'll be herself."

Joel helped Mother clean the dishes. Outside, the storm crashed around them. Issachar had brought Laban and Dodo before the worst of it, but now they would not be still, but fidgeted in their stalls. Joel wondered how Hamor and Gaddiel were doing.

The wind and lightning must be much terrible in unprotected pastures.

There was not much to do after the dishes were put away and the cooking area set in order. Usually, the evening meant sitting outdoors or visiting neighbors. Not tonight. No one with any sense would be anywhere except at home.

Everyone went to bed early. Joel carried Ta-Muit up the ladder and put her beside Miriam, who did not rouse. A woven mat had been affixed over the window, but some rain, blown by the fierce winds, came into the room anyway. Thunder crashed and lightning flared up, then disappeared, only to be replaced by the next flash.

He slept what seemed a long time but was awakened by Ta-Muit pawing him in the face. She would not settle, even when he petted her and whispered that she must sleep. She purred, but it was not the sound of contentment. No, there was something urgent in the noises she was making. Then the cat went to the ladder and meowed most piteously.

"What is it?" Joel whispered. "Are you frightened of the storm? It's nothing. We're safe here. In the morning, the rain will be over and everything will be fine. You'll see."

But Ta-Muit would not stop. She kept looking into the room below and pawing at the top of the ladder. Clearly, she wanted to go down. Then it occurred to Joel that the cat was about to have her kittens. Maybe she wanted the bed Miriam had made for her.

Joel gave in. "All right," he told her. "Let's go." He carried her, making sure at every step that his footing was secure. Downstairs, he put Ta-Muit on her bed, but she was not content. Instead, she went to the door and began meowing and pawing at it, just as she had done earlier.

"No!" Joel whispered. "You can't go outside. Not in this storm."

She would not be denied. "You won't like it," Joel warned. But when he opened the door, she went through, turned, and gave him such a look of pleading that he felt she needed him. It was nearly dawn, and despite the terrible storm, there was some light in the sky, just enough to see a little distance.

Needed him to do what? King Solomon's words came to him: "You have the gift. You speak the language of the animals."

"What is it? What can I do?"

The cat took a few steps up the street, turned, looked back, and mewed pitifully.

Then he knew. "You want me to come with you?"

By way of answer, Ta-Muit scampered into the gloom. In a moment, he lost sight of her.

"Wait!" Joel called after her. He closed the door behind him. Already he was drenched and he realized he was barefoot. He should go back inside, find dry clothes, and go to his sleeping mat without waking his family.

That was the sensible thing to do.

That was not what he did.

Twenty-five

Instead, he started up the street. "Ta-Muit!" he called. "Where are you?" Then he saw her, waiting for him. When he caught up with her, she started off again, pushing her way through darkness and storm to . . .

Where, he could not guess. He himself was having to feel his way. Flashes of lightning lit up the sky and allowed him to run a few steps at a time. Always up ahead he could hear Ta-Muit meowing, and once his eyes became accustomed to the dim light, he could see her, leading him onward.

The cat moved with steady purpose up the street leading to Joel's school, the palace, and beyond that, the temple. Joel could hardly keep up. Rain poured down over his face and his clothes stuck to him. He was shivering, both because it was cold and because he was frightened by the storm. *I should go back,* he kept thinking. *Why am I doing this?*

He already knew that one way or another, he was soon going to be in terrible trouble. What if his family had already waked up and discovered that he was gone? His mother would be terrified to think that he was out in the storm—and for what reason? Father would insist on searching for him. And when he found him . . .

Now they were at the palace. The gates were shut. Joe's foot slipped on a wet paving stone, and he felt down on his knees, scraping the right one so badly that he knew it was bleeding. He pushed himself up and continued. Now he could make out the wall surrounding the temple. Ta-Muit kept on. Joel came to the massive eastern gate and in a flash of lightning saw that it was open, just barely. The cat slipped through and was gone. Joel followed. Why were the gates open on such a night, even just a crack? His cat had found her way. He'd followed her this far: would he stop now?

Everything sensible told him *yes!* It was time to leave Ta-Muit to herself. She knew where she was going and what she was doing. She always did. The gates were open enough to let her pass, so she was meant to find her way into YAH's temple. But what about himself?

Joel felt the opening. To his amazement, he realized he was thin enough to slip through, just as Ta-Muit had done.

Stop! all the voices inside him cried out. The voices of his parents, his grandfather, Elishama, even Benjamin and Issachar. He had no right to enter the temple courtyard like this, not during this terrible storm.

But Ta-Muit was somewhere inside, and she needed him. That's why she'd led him all this way.

Joel slipped through and then he was in the vast, deserted courtyard. Any moment he expected that the temple guards would see him, and then his hands would be tied; he would be taken to the guardhouse while they decided what to do with him.

But there were no guards. The torches on the inner walls were nothing more than sticks, their fires long since extinguished by the rain. Joel scanned the open space, straining to find Ta-Muit. There she was, heading directly for the temple itself and its towering doors. He followed. "Ta-Muit!" he began calling. "Come back! Come to me!" There was no one to hear, and if there were, it would just hasten the moment he was caught. If she heard him, the cat did not obey. She scampered up the steps leading to the doors, which, to Joel's astonishment, were open too. Not fully, but just a little, like the outer gates. What was going on? Was the temple guarded no better than this, even on a night of storm?

Joel ran to the bottom step. On its tall stone platform, the temple loomed above him. And here he was, small, soaked and shivering, daring even to think of entering. But his cat was inside, and he'd followed her this far. He was already in the most horrible predicament of his life, so what more could he do to make things even worse?

Before he could talk himself out of it, Joel climbed the stairs, and followed Ta-Muit into the house of YAH.

Now I will be struck dead, was his first thought. But nothing happened. Raindrops poured off him, making a puddle on the smooth stones. It was a relief to be sheltered from the storm. It was warmer here than outside, too. Joel was still shivering, but now as much from fear and excitement as he was from the cold.

Then he looked around, and what he saw caused him to drop to his knees. This was the Holy Place, and it was full of splendor, as befitting the God of Israel. The walls gleamed, for they were of gold leaf pressed over carved images of palm trees, flowers, and frightening creatures with the bodies of lions, wings of eagles, and heads of human beings. In the middle of the chamber stood a golden altar. Joel knew this was where the priests offered daily sacrifices of blood, incense, and food. On either side, along the golden walls, stood seven-branched candlesticks, all lighted. Their flames bathed the room in a golden glow.

Joel remembered how the upland pastures in their springtime beauty had made him think that the Garden of Eden must have looked like them. But here was an image of Eden beyond anything he had ever imagined. And here he was, Joel ben-Nathan, alone in the place where YAH dwelt.

Well, not quite alone. Familiar meowing caught his attention. He looked. Ta-Muit stood by the bottom of the steps leading up to the Holy of Holies. Then she climbed them and disappeared behind the embroidered scarlet curtain that separated the Holy Place from the most sacred chamber that lay beyond it, where YAH himself sat enthroned above the ark of the covenant, which was protected by the mighty cherubim, said to be gigantic figures whose outspread wings touched the walls and also sheltered the ark itself.

Ta-Muit might dare to enter the Holy of Holies, but he, Joel, would not. Only the High Priest was permitted to enter, and that on only one day a year, the Day of Atonement. For anyone else to enter must bring death, for no one could look on YAH and live.

Here he was, then, a trespasser in the temple. What would he say when he was caught, for he knew that he would be. *My cat ran in here and I had to follow?* What fool would believe such a fantastic tale?

Outside the temple, the storm was dying down. Soon, the priests would appear for the morning rituals. The guards, who had probably sought shelter from the storm last night, would take up their assigned stations. And he would be discovered and thrown into some lightless cell in a deep prison.

I could try and escape now, he thought. *No one needs to find out what I've done. Ta-Muit can look after herself.*

Unable to decide, he went to the front right corner of the Holy Place, sat, pulled up his knees, and tried to make himself as small as possible. He was still shivering, needed a latrine, and dreaded the punishment that would surely come to him later.

And then there was Ta-Muit. Was she even alive now, or had she incurred the penalty for any living thing that dared enter the Holy of Holies? And if Ta-Muit were dead, what about her kittens?

Soon, Joel heard the doors to the Holy Place being pushed open and then some raised voices. He couldn't make out precisely what was being said, but he gathered that someone was angry with someone else that neither the gates between the street and the outer court, nor the doors into the temple itself, had been securely closed last night. He heard a man's voice try and explain something about the storm and how no one would dare be outside amid the cloudbursts and thunder and lightning.

No one except a spotted Egyptian cat and me, Joel thought. For some reason, it made him smile to think such a thing.

The doors opened and several priests entered, some carrying flasks of oil. It would be their job to refill the golden candlesticks. Others had brooms, and it occurred to Joel that even YAH's house needed sweeping. That made him smile, too. Still others went to the golden altar to prepare it for the morning sacrifice.

Joel waited to be discovered. It didn't take long. A sneeze saw to that.

Twenty-six

In an instant, guards surrounded him. "Who are you?" one demanded. He seemed to be the one in charge. "What are you doing, profaning the temple?"

"Get up!" a second guard ordered.

Joel was yanked to his feet. By now, the commotion had attracted the priests, who hurried to see what was going on.

"What's happening?" one asked.

"Sacrilege!" another exclaimed.

"Look at me!" the head guard ordered.

Joel did.

"Why are you here? Answer, if you value your life!"

Joel could see no reason not to tell the truth. "My cat woke me in the night and wanted to go out. I followed her, and she led me here. The doors were open, and she came through, and so did I. She went behind the veil of the Holy of Holies. She must be there now."

This account was met with astounded silence.

"You're lying!" the guard said. "Tell us the real reason you are here."

"I *am* telling the truth," Joel insisted. "I couldn't invent such a story."

"And this cat, you say, has dared to enter the Most Holy Place?" a priest asked.

"Yes, sir. I saw her."

"Swear it by YAH!"

"I swear."

"The boy's mad," another priest suggested. "He doesn't know what he's saying. Tell us who you are," he commanded.

"I am Joel ben-Nathan. My father is the scribe Nathan ben-Eliezer. My grandfather is the priest Eliezer."

The priests looked at each other. "Eliezer," one said. "If the boy's story is true, Eliezer must be told."

"He knows about my cat," Joel told them. "So does the king. He's waiting for her kittens to be born because he wishes to present two of them to Queen Isetnofret."

"He lies!" the head guard accused.

"Perhaps," said the priest. "But we've heard about the cat that was brought before the king and that a boy, the animal's master, was His Majesty's guest in his private garden. There might be truth in what the lad says."

"He belongs in the prison," the guard countered.

"That's not our decision. Send for Eliezer," the priest told one of his fellows. "We'll let him decide what to do."

"And in the meantime?" the guard asked the priest.

"We wait."

"Here?"

The priest gave this some thought. "No. Take the boy to your post. He's wet and cold. See if you can find him something dry to put on and get him something hot to drink. And send one of your men to the house of Nathan ben-Eliezer and tell him to come immediately. The family must be sick with worry."

Joel had forgotten that. But of course, by this time, his parents and sister were awake and wondering where he and Ta-Muit had gone. Shame washed over him. Making them worry was the last thing he wanted.

"Dry clothes? Hot food? You want us to pamper him?" the guard said. "He's a prisoner, not a guest!"

"He's a child," the priest said. "Anyone can see he's exhausted and frightened."

The priest was right. Joel could not stop shaking. The priest was kind, and he didn't think that the guards, for all that they were scary looking and rough spoken, would actually harm him. No, he feared someone else: his grandfather.

"Come with me," the guard ordered. He seized Joel by the shoulder, and his grip was like iron. Joel was half-pulled from the Holy Place, through the now-open gates, into the courtyard, and then into a side chamber of the temple which the guards used when on duty.

The guard found a dry tunic for Joel. It felt wonderful to be out of wet clothes, and although the tunic was twice as large as he needed, he was grateful for it. Food was brought, including a hot stew; no other broth had ever tasted as good. Before long, his feet and hands were warm, and he felt sleep coming over him. But just as his head was nodding, Grandfather marched into the room.

Joel sprang to his feet. "YAH be with you, Grandfather."

Grandfather did not return the blessing. "What do I hear? You let your cat violate the holiness of the temple? An unclean animal in the Holy Place? Tell me it's a delirium—or a lie! Either would be better than what you've told these guards and my priests!"

"I did tell the truth, Grandfather. It happened just as I told them. Ta-Muit woke me up. She wanted to go outside—"

"In the storm? Impossible! Even I know that cats hate to be wet."

"She *did* want to. I opened the door, thinking she would come back, but instead, she looked at me, and I could tell she wanted me to follow her."

"You still insist you can understand the animals—is that it?"

"She came here, to the temple. The outer gates were open enough to let us through, and so were the doors to the temple."

"Someone will be punished for that," Grandfather declared.

"Ta-Muit went in, and I followed her."

"You had no right!" Grandfather exclaimed. "You are not a priest!"

"I know. But I was afraid for my cat."

"Where is the creature now?"

"She ran up the steps to the Holy of Holies and went behind the curtain."

Grandfather staggered as if he'd been struck with a rod of iron. "That's what I was told, but I refused to believe it! The Holy of Holies profaned! And by . . . "

He could not bring himself to finish his thought, but Joel understood well what he was thinking: "a *cat*."

At that moment, Father burst into the room. He gathered Joel into his arms. "Thanks be to YAH that you're safe! We couldn't imagine where you'd gone."

"He swears that he followed that cat here," Grandfather broke in.

"YAH be with you," Father told him.

Again, Grandfather offered no return blessing. "And your son further declares that the beast entered into the Holy Place and then . . . "

"Not into the Holy of Holies?" Father asked. "Surely not! Joel?"

"I saw her go there," he whispered.

"It's not possible," Father muttered.

"I'm starting to believe that *anything* is possible with that animal," Grandfather retorted. "Anything!"

Father looked carefully at Joel. "You're certain of this?"

"Yes, sir."

"And you're not telling us a tale? If you are, it's not funny."

"No, sir! It's what happened."

"Very well. What do we do now?"

Everyone looked at Grandfather. He wasn't the high priest, nor was he the king. The decision wasn't his to make, but there was no one else who could. Joel could see that his grandfather was now not as angry as he was weary—and worried.

Finally, he spoke. "I should inform the high priest, but he is ill with a fever."

"Miriam was ill, as well," Father said.

"And how is she?" Grandfather asked.

"Much better. The physician says she will recover."

"Many in Jerusalem are sick, and some have died. The high priest is very sick, and he is old. He doesn't need to be bothered with this."

"What about the king?" Father asked.

"The temple is not his to rule! No, we will deal with this matter ourselves. Do you agree?" Grandfather asked his fellow priests.

"Yes, sir," they said.

"What will you do?" Father asked.

"If the animal is indeed in the Holy of Holies, she is most likely dead. YAH will not have his dwelling profaned by unclean beasts."

"Sir," one of the other priests said, "if that is true, we cannot permit her body to decay in the Holy of Holies. That would make it unclean."

"The holiness of YAH can purify all uncleanness, if necessary, but you are right, Paltiel."

"Yet no one can enter the Holy of Holies except the high priest on the Day of Atonement."

"It is a problem," Grandfather agreed.

Joel listened to the men discussing the matter; no one had sent him from the guard chamber. He was being treated like a man, his presence unquestioned if not noticed, even by his grandfather. This thought gave him courage to speak up. "Let me go back into the Holy Place and call her. If Ta-Muit is alive, she'll come to me."

Grandfather looked doubtful, perhaps still unconvinced that Joel had the power to speak to animals and bend them to his will.

"What do you think?" Joel's father asked. "It might work."

"Very well. We will try it. And you, Joel, had better pray that your cat will obey you—if she still lives."

Twenty-seven

THEY left the guardhouse and made for the temple. Men were gathering for the morning sacrifice, and Joel noticed them staring, no doubt wondering what he was doing there and why he and his father were being allowed inside the temple.

The guards left them at the doors, so now it was Grandfather, Father, Joel, and three priests. Once again, the beauty of the room overwhelmed him, and Joel heard his father gasp at the sight of the golden walls, the raised images of trees and flowers and mysterious winged creatures.

At the far end of the chamber, the crimson curtain hung before the doors to the Holy of Holies. They approached, and with each step, Joel found himself trembling all the more. He was not a priest. He was not yet a grown man. Yet here he was, blessed to see what only a few men of Israel would ever behold, the beauty of YAH's temple. What a story he would have for Benjamin and Issachar!

"Halt," Grandfather ordered when they had come to the steps to the Holy of Holies.

All the men stood in silence. The room smelled faintly of burning oil and incense. Pale light filtered through windows high in the side walls.

Joel knew the others were looking at him, expecting him to say something. "May I?" he asked Grandfather. The old man nodded.

"Ta-Muit!" Joel called softly. "Ta-Muit, come to me. It's Joel."

They waited. Nothing.

"Ta-Muit!" Joel called again. "It's Joel. Come out. We'll go home."

Still nothing.

Grandfather let out a deep breath. "Either the cat is dead or the boy simply imagined she came into the temple. Perhaps he has fever, too, and it makes him see deceiving visions."

Grandfather was wrong, but this was no time to argue. "Ta-Muit," Joel called again. "Come out! It's all right. We'll go home."

The heavy crimson curtain rustled, and there appeared first a tawny head with the mark of a scarab above the golden eyes, the long white whiskers, and the white patch under the throat. It was Ta-Muit.

Joel wanted to sob with relief. "Come!" he called.

The cat stepped from behind the curtain, and now all of her was visible: the long black stripe down her back and extending to the tip of her tail, the spotted bronze coat. And there was something in her mouth.

"Not a rat," Joel prayed. "Not in the temple of YAH."

"Come," he urged again.

Ta-Muit began her way down the steps.

"Joel, get her!" Grandfather commanded.

"No, wait!" Father said. "Look what she has."

Without asking permission, Joel hurried to the cat and knelt before her. Father was right: it was no rat in Ta-Muit's mouth.

It was a kitten.

A tiny, blind, mewing thing with a coat the color of ripening wheat.

Ta-Muit brushed past Joel and proceeded to where his grandfather stood silent and unmoving. She laid her baby at his feet, as if she were the queen of Sheba presenting the King of Israel with a treasure beyond price.

The baby squirmed and cried, its tiny voice the only sound in the golden room.

Then before anyone could seize her, Ta-Muit scampered back up the steps, disappeared behind the curtain, and immediately returned with another kitten. This one, a little larger than the first, was pure black, as black as the lines drawn around an Egyptian maiden's eyes. She also presented it to Grandfather, then turned and hurried back up the steps. Ta-Muit repeated these movements until six mewing babies lay at Grandfather's feet. The whole time, he had neither moved nor spoken.

When Ta-Muit made no sign that she needed to return to the Holy of Holies, Father was the first to speak. "Can someone find us a basket?" he asked, addressing himself to one of the priests. "I am certain that these little ones need to nurse. A bare stone floor is not a fitting place for them."

"May I?" a priest asked Grandfather.

He nodded.

Joel knelt by the babies. He picked them up, one by one. Two were pure black. Two were marked like their mother. Swirls of black, brown, and gold covered the sides of the fifth, and the last, the tiniest of them all, was gold. Ta-Muit stayed by him, licking her babies, who tried to nestle against her belly so they could nurse. All the while, she purred and allowed Joel to stroke her.

The priest returned with a large wicker basket. Joel lifted Ta-Muit into it, and then her babies, one by one.

"What now?" Father asked.

All this time, Grandfather had still not spoken. Joel could not tell what he was feeling. Would he order the priest to take the cats and drown them? After all, they had desecrated the most holy place in Israel. Even Joel knew that birth made a mother unclean until she could be purified, and here was a cat, itself unclean, having committed the ultimate act of sacrilege.

"Take them to the priests' dwelling," Grandfather replied. "We will care for them there."

"Do you mean it, Grandfather?" he asked. "You're not going to . . . " He couldn't finish his thought.

"Kill them?" Grandfather responded. "No, even though I do not approve of anything you and this cat have done."

"Clearly not," Father said.

Grandfather let that pass. "You shouldn't have allowed the animal out into the storm," he began. "You should not have followed her. Instead, you should have wakened your father and mother and let them decide what to do. You put yourself in danger by being out in the storm alone. You should not have followed the cat into the temple courtyard, and you should not have gone into the temple! Do you agree with all I have said?"

Joel glanced at his father, hoping he would speak to defend him. But Father said nothing, only looked back at him, his left eyebrow raised higher than Joel had ever seen it.

"I'm waiting for you answer," Grandfather told him.

"You are right in everything you have said," Joel admitted.

"Did you know you were doing wrong?"

Something in Joel wanted to say that he had done the *right* thing; Ta-Muit needed him, and it was his responsibility to care for her. But this was no time for excuses. In everyone else's mind, he had made one horrible decision after another.

"Did you know?" Grandfather demanded.

Joel could not meet his eyes. "Yes, sir."

"The cat and its kittens should rightfully be put to death, and you should be punished severely for daring enter the temple."

"Yes, sir."

Grandfather sighed. "Be glad that I am not the supreme power in Israel, for everything in me wants to be rid of these pests forever. If I were your father, I would have you removed from your school and put out to work at hard labor until you could learn the lesson of obedience to the laws of YAH and of your elders."

"Yes, sir," Joel whispered.

"But I bow to a power higher than myself," Grandfather went on. "By rights, the cat should have been struck dead for entering the Holy of Holies. But YAH is merciful. He allowed his dwelling to be invaded by this—" the old man struggled to find the words he wanted—"this *maker of mischief*! If YAH did not prefer to have an unclean beast in his house, he nevertheless allowed her to enter without penalty. Perhaps he loves the creatures he has made more than we do. I don't pretend to know his will, but if he has favored this cat and her kittens, far be it from me to exact judgment and punishment where YAH has blessed new life."

Joel wanted to throw his arms around his grandfather and sob his thanks, but he suspected it would cause embarrassment. Besides, he had no words to express what he was feeling. Later, he might figure it all out, but for now, there was one clear thing in his mind: Ta-Muit and her kittens would live.

"You are wise and compassionate," Father told Grandfather.

"Enough of such flattery!" Grandfather exclaimed. "Take these creatures and see that they are well cared for." His voice was gruff, but his expression had softened.

"May I go with them?" Joel asked.

Grandfather threw up his hands. "Why not? You've already broken nearly all the rules of this place. Yes, go! It's time for the morning sacrifice, and we don't need stray cats and boys where they should not be."

"I must go home and tell your mother and sister what has happened," Father told Joel. "I will also inform Elishama that you will be late for school."

Joel followed the priest to the house where others like himself lived during their term of temple service. The basket full of cats was placed in a safe corner. The kittens began nursing right away, and the priest assured Joel that they would all be cared for.

"You should go home," the priest advised him. "Your mother will want to see you with her own eyes. Besides, you need rest."

"You'll look after them?" Joel asked.

The priest smiled. "I promise. Come back later. By then, someone will have decided what's to be done."

"Please remind Grandfather that the king commanded two kittens to be the price of Ta-Muit's killing of his partridges," Joel said.

The priest nodded. "I will. Don't worry. No harm will come to your cats."

Twenty-eight

Mother made a big fuss over Joel—after scolding him for giving her the fright of her life. She cried a little, had him change into his own clothes, and insisted that he go to the loft and rest. For his part, Joel was glad to be home. He was frantic for sleep, but he couldn't stop thinking about all that had happened. Then he began to feel feverish. After a while, he felt as though he were on fire. He called for Mother, whose face told him how sick he looked. She ordered Miriam to fetch the physician. By the time he arrived, Joel was drenched with his own sweat, and he kept seeing Ta-Muit before his eyes, running away from him into a black whirlwind. In his delirium, Joel tried to follow, and Mother had to hold his shoulders to the sleeping mat and sponge his forehead at the same time.

Later, they told him how the physician had come, given him medicine, helped restrain him while he moaned and cried out for Ta-Muit and tried to tear off his tunic, crying that he was burning up from the flames of the candlesticks in the Holy Place. He remembered none of it. When he finally woke up and felt better, Father told him he had been lost in fever for two days. Someone had been with him all that time. Grandfather had come and sat praying for hours, asking YAH to heal Joel—to spare his life. That's how bad the fever had been.

When at last Joel came to himself and his life was no longer in danger, he felt as helpless and weak as Ta-Muit's kittens. Mother made him rest; he was not permitted even to descend the ladder and join the family for meals. Everything was brought to him. By the fifth day, he felt much better, well enough to wonder how the cats were faring and eager to see them for himself. But Father pointed out that Joel had done enough of going to places where he had not been invited. The king, Father believed, would send for Joel in his own time.

And that's what happened.

Joel was sitting up on his mat, drinking cool water, when there was a knock on the door. Mother answered, and Joel strained to hear what was being said. When she came up the ladder, she was beaming.

"Who was it, Mother?"

"A messenger from the palace. You are asked to come and see how Ta-Muit and her kittens are doing. In fact, all of us are commanded to appear before the king!"

This was great news beyond Joel's imagining. "When?"

Mother's eyes sparkled. The care and tiredness that had marked her face during the past days were gone, replaced by joy. "Tomorrow! A messenger from the palace will call for us after the mid-day meal."

"All of us?" Joel was having a hard time grasping what Mother was saying.

"Yes!"

"Me, too?" Miriam said.

"Yes, my darling! We will meet your father there, since he will already be at his work."

"I wonder if Grandfather knows," Joel said.

Mother smiled. "If he doesn't know already, he will soon enough. Perhaps this will put an end to his grumbling."

That made Joel smile, too.

"There's much to be done," Mother went on. "We need to look our best, and that means clean clothes, baths for all of us—your Father's hair needs cutting and so does yours, Joel. Perhaps your sister and I can have Deborah arrange our hair."

"Can I wear my new necklace and bracelet?" Miriam asked.

Mother took her hands and twirled her around. "Of course, Little Star! You will be as beautiful as any of the young girls at the palace."

Mother turned to Joel. "I can't remember being this excited since—well, since the day your father and I were married."

"Everything's turned out all right, hasn't it?" Joel asked. Suddenly, he felt ashamed. "I'm sorry for all the trouble I've caused. And Ta-Muit, too. I never meant to worry you and Father."

Mother hugged him. "You did give us quite a turn. And not because of what you and Ta-Muit did the night it stormed. I mean when you were so sick with fever. Nothing is more important than your recovery—yours and Miriam's, too."

"I want to see Ta-Muit's babies," Miriam said. "Can I play with them?"

"They're too small right now," Mother reminded her. "Perhaps you can hold one, if Ta-Muit allows it."

"Will she, Joel?" Miriam asked.

"I think so."

And Ta-Muit did allow it. The family met at the palace the next day and were escorted to the same courtyard where the king had spoken with Joel. He felt humble and thankful that all the upset Ta-Muit had caused was resulting in this honor that few citizens of Israel would ever receive.

Miriam took it all in with wide eyes. While they waited for someone to bring Ta-Muit and her kittens, she walked around the courtyard, staring at the birds on their perches, the monkeys, the mongooses. But she could not tear herself away from the two cheetahs, both of which came to the bars of their cage and eyed her with great interest. Joel wondered if they looked at Miriam as a friend or something good to eat.

Mother kept exclaiming over the palm trees in pots, the vines covered with scarlet and white blooms, the water lilies in the fountain. Father just stood and beamed at his family, enjoying their wonderment.

Joel kept expecting a servant to appear with Ta-Muit and her kittens, but he was not prepared to see King Solomon himself enter the courtyard, followed by servants, two bearing a large basket from which came the tiny mewing of kittens. Ta-Muit herself walked beside the king, her eyes fixed on the basket.

Behind the king, Queen Isetnofret appeared, followed by two of her handmaidens. She was dressed as Joel had seen her before, but this time, her gown was blue, tied with a richly beaded belt. Her wig was elaborated braided, and a diadem of gold sat on top of that.

She's dressed to look her best, too, Joel thought, and he felt honored. It came to him that his mother and sister had done the same. He glanced at the queen and then at his mother, and with pride he felt that his mother was just as beautiful as the younger woman.

Everyone in the family knelt.

"Welcome, friends," the king greeted. "Rise."

Father bowed. "Your Majesty," he began. "We are honored to be summoned into your presence. May I present my wife, Adah, and my daughter, Miriam. I believe you already know my son, Joel."

The king looked at Joel and a faint smile played over his face. "Joel the trespasser," he declared. "Joel the cat-follower. Joel the lion-hearted, brave enough to enter the house of YAH without being invited."

Joel bowed his head. "I am sorry, Your Majesty. I know I have done wrong and deserve your strict judgment."

"YAH himself has pronounced judgment, my son, and has declared you not guilty. If YAH had been angry with you and your cat, you would not be here today."

"Our God is most merciful," Father added. "Your Majesty likewise."

Ta-Muit must have lost patience with all these high-sounding words, for she pawed at the leg of the servants holding the basket. At the king's nod, they put it down, and Ta-Muit went to it. But she did not settle down to nurse. Instead, she went to Joel, and looked at him expectantly.

"May I?" he asked the king.

Solomon nodded. “Of course. She *is* your cat.”

Joel picked her up. Immediately, she began to purr.

Queen Isetnofret came forward. The family bowed to her, too.

“You’re so pretty,” Miriam told her.

The king translated. The queen replied in Egyptian.

“My lady thanks you. She says your necklace is beautiful and wants to know if you bought it in Egypt.”

“No, sir. Egyptian traders came to Jerusalem. Mama bought it for me. They brought Ta-Muit, too.”

The queen had knelt by the basket of kittens; she gestured to Miriam to come have a closer look. In a moment, the two were chatting, no matter that they did not speak each other’s language.

“Mother, come look!” Miriam said.

Mother joined them, and in a moment, all three were exclaiming over the kittens, inspecting them one by one.

King Solomon nodded his approval. Then he addressed Father. “A word with you, Nathan ben-Eliezer.”

“Yes, Sire,” Father told him.

“Come with me, then. Joel, stay here and enjoy some time with your cat. She’s missed you greatly. She told me so.”

The king walked into the middle of the courtyard, where the fountain splashed. Father followed, and they spoke with one another.

Joel couldn’t tell what they were saying, but it didn’t matter. He knew he would forever remember this moment. Never could he have imagined that he would be in King Solomon’s palace, holding a cat, while his mother and sister joined the Egyptian Queen of Israel in playing with six tiny kittens.

After a while, Father called for Joel. “Let Ta-Muit stay with her kittens,” he said.

Joel put her down, and she went to the basket, climbed in, and immediately was besieged by six hungry babies.

Father looked serious. “His Majesty has been telling me about your last conversation.”

“Yes, sir. I told you about it.”

"Not that you shared with His Majesty your unhappiness about being trained as a scribe, or your desire to be a shepherd."

"No, sir."

"And why not?"

"I didn't mean to complain! It just came out while we were talking."

"I asked your son about himself," the king said. "I could tell he's not happy. YAH has given me the gift of seeing into men's hearts. Your son was honest enough to let me know that what I read in him is correct."

"You should have told me what you shared with His Majesty," Father said.

"I'm sorry. I meant no disrespect."

"Did you tell His Majesty my decision about your future training?"

"I don't remember."

"Tell him now."

Joel wanted to run, but there was nowhere he could hide. He had to answer. "My father told me that one day my feelings will change and I will be glad he made me finish my training. I can never be a shepherd."

"That is your father's wish, and you must obey."

"Yes, Your Majesty."

"However, your father and I have been talking. He wants what is best for you, and he has agreed to a plan that you might accept."

"My Lord?"

"You have the gift of understanding the animals. I saw it in you the moment I met you and Ta-Muit. A man should be able to follow his heart, but you also have the duty to obey your father, as I obeyed my father's wish that I become king. Your teacher, Elishama, tells me you are a gifted scribe, and that reading comes easily to you."

"You spoke to him about me?"

"I did. You have been much on my mind, Joel ben-Nathan. You and your cat. You have three gifts: one for understanding the ways and language of the animals, one for writing, and one for drawing."

"Elishama informed you of that?" Father asked.

"He did. And he said he was sorry that there is no place in Israel for such a gift."

"May I speak freely?" Father asked. The king nodded. "Then let me remind Your Majesty that the walls of the Holy Place are decorated with images of trees and blossoms and cherubim."

The king smiled. "Indeed. And they're beautiful, are they not?"

"More beautiful than any other thing I have ever seen."

"I know YAH's distaste for graven images, yet He revealed to us how he wanted his house to be decorated." The king paused while he looked at Father. "You are wise enough to see the seeming contradiction. So am I. But beyond that, it's not been revealed to me how to resolve it. Perhaps you have a suggestion?"

Joel realized that the king had just paid his father a great compliment.

"At this moment, nothing comes to me," Father replied. "But should YAH reveal to me his will in the matter, I will send word—if Your Majesty so wishes it."

"I do wish it, and I thank you for your service." The king turned his attention to Joel. "Here is what I've proposed to your father. You must obey him and continue at school. But I suggest that two or three times each week, after your training for the day is completed, you come here and assist my servants who care for my—pets. You will learn much, and I don't mean from their keepers, but from the animals themselves. Besides, I want Ta-Muit and her kittens to remain here until they are weaned, and you will want time with them."

Joel's heart sang. What the king proposed was more than he could have dreamed. He also guessed that King Solomon would not have mentioned his plan unless Father had already agreed to it.

"My Lord is most gracious."

"You approve, then?" the king replied.

"Yes, My Lord."

"I have one other thing to suggest, and your father agrees. Once in a while, you should go with your friend the shepherd—what is his name?—"

"Issachar."

"Issachar, into the pastures to help care for the sheep. You should stay some nights, too. My father often told us how his life as a shepherd was the best training for kingship that he ever had, even better than being taught how to bear arms or plan battle strategies. Perhaps your father would join you sometimes." The king looked at Father. "What do you say?"

Father bowed his head. "With all my heart."

"It's done, then," the king declared. "I will have my scribes write it down."

Joel wanted to dance. To embrace his father. Even to embrace the king, but it would be unseemly. Instead, he got down on one knee and said, "I thank you, My Lord. I pledge you my life."

The king chuckled. "Enough of that! Let's leave such high-flown words to my counselors."

Joel stood. The king looked him in the eye. "I thank you for the kittens. My lady has chosen the two she wants. When they're weaned, you will leave them here for her, but the others are yours to do with as you like. Ta-Muit, as well. I don't know if your mother will want five cats in her house. My mother would not! When they are grown, you will have many more."

Father sighed. "Can Your Majesty suggest what we should do with them all?"

The king shook his head. "My only wisdom is this: cats have returned to Jerusalem, thanks to your son."

"And to the Egyptian traders," Father said.

"And to Ta-Muit," Joel added.

Twenty-Nine

Queen Isetnofret chose for herself one of the pure black kittens and the one with swirls of black, brown, and white on its sides. That left the other black kitten, the two tawny spotted ones, and the little one who was all gold. That one became Miriam's favorite. Father said it was a female, so Miriam named her Abigail, in honor of the wisest of all King David's wives. Joel named the others: the black one, a male, he called Kush. The two tawny ones, who appeared to be twins, he named Jacob and Esau.

From the day his family visited the king in his palace, Joel began to spend three afternoons each week among the king's pets. Ta-Muit and her kittens were usually there, and sometimes, Joel met the queen. The king he did not see.

When the kittens were weaned, Queen Isetnofret took her cats for her own. She thanked Joel many times, and through an interpreter, let him know how much joy they had brought her, and how with them near her, she felt less homesick for her family.

Then it was time to bring Ta-Muit and the other kittens home. The whole family went to the palace for the event, and when they left—Joel and Father sharing the weight of a large basket full of cats, Miriam holding Abigail in her arms, and Ta-Muit leading the way—it seemed that half of Jerusalem had turned out to watch the spectacle and welcome them home.

Life would never be the same, but it soon settled into its new routine. Joel's yearning for a different life was satisfied. He would not, perhaps, travel to strange countries and see their wonders—at least not right away. Surprisingly, his life in Jerusalem contented him. Every time he went to the palace to help care for the animals, he tried with all his might to understand their speech, whether their words were growls, howls, snorts, or simply silent watching.

He sometimes went with Issachar into the hills to tend the sheep, and a few times, Father joined them. They spent some nights around Hamor and Gaddiel's campfire, laughing at Hamor's outrageous tales. Joel learned some things he might not otherwise have know until he was older, but Father did not make much fuss about it. He said Joel was a man, and men liked to tell and listen to stories, even some that were . . .

Once in a while, when he and Issachar were tending the flock near the sandy place where there were not jagged rocks, Joel would draw pictures. Some he copied from what was around him. Some he drew from memory. Issachar especially liked the images of the cherubim Joel had seen on the walls of the Holy Place. He could hardly believe that creatures with the bodies of lions, the wings of eagles, and the heads of human actually existed. Joel told him he thought they were just imaginary, but Issachar had trouble understanding how anything could be imagined if it were not also real.

At school, Joel felt satisfied. He worked hard at his lessons, and he learned how to read anything that was put in front of him. Taking accurate dictation took more time, but Elishama was pleased with his progress. These skills made him proud, for not even the king possessed them. But Joel kept that a secret, as he kept secret all that Solomon had told him of his unhappiness and the hardships of being a king.

Grandfather sometimes came to the house, and while he did not fancy all the cats, he allowed that things had turned out better than he had expected. While he did not agree with how YAH had decided the fate of Ta-Muit and her kittens, he bowed to the power and will of the God of Israel.

Then the Egyptians traders reappeared in Jerusalem, heading south to Egypt after months spent in the cities far to the north. The day they arrived, Joel asked his father to come with him to the marketplace while he looked for Seb. Father agreed. It didn't take any time to find him. The boy was a little taller, perhaps, a little less bony. He was still under the power of his master, and he was still made to sing and dance for the crowds.

Joel had many questions for Seb. He was glad Father was with him, since Father knew enough Egyptian to act as translator. Then Seb's master appeared, so there was no question now that everyone would be able to understand everyone else.

Seb acted glad to see Joel, and he had questions himself. "Did you find my cat?" was the first one.

Joel told him yes, and then, with Father and the Egyptian trader communicating his story, he explained everything.

The Egyptian dared to suggest that Joel fetch Ta-Muit so she could be returned to her rightful owner. Father put a quick end to that possibility by reminding him how King Solomon himself had settled matters.

Seb, for his part, was happy to hear Joel's story. "Ta-Muit wanted to stay with you, and she did," he said simply. "Cats can and will do whatever they like."

Joel had to agree.

Then Seb had a surprise. He went into the tent and came back with—

Two cats! Both gray, the color of smoke. A male and a female, Seb said in answer to Father's question.

"From Persia," Seb explained. "To replace Ta-Muit. I will take them home with me to Egypt."

Joel had an idea. "Come with us to our house. You can see Ta-Muit again. She can meet your new cats."

"May I?" Seb asked his master.

"If you return immediately. You have work to do this evening."

Seb put his cats into a basket and they walked to Joel's house. Inside, with the door shut, Seb opened it and there was a grand meeting. Ta-Muit came to Seb immediately; it was plain that she remembered him. But she growled at the gray Persians, the larger of which Seb said was named Rustum. That did not last long, and soon, she was nuzzling the male, and he was indicating his definite interest in her.

Miriam introduced Abigail, Kush, Jacob, and Esau to the gray cats, and after some suspicious sniffing and growling, they all acted friendly.

"Seven cats!" Mother exclaimed. "Six too many!"

"Mama," Miriam wailed. "What about Abigail?"

Joel saw how Ta-Muit and the male Persian were behaving with one another. He also knew that his mother was already worn out with having so many animals in the house. Laban and Dodo feared the cats and began bleating every time one came too near their pens. There never seemed to be a quiet moment anymore. What could be done?

Then Joel had an idea.

"Seb," he began. "If it's all right with my mother and father, you could leave Rustum here. Ta-Muit needs a mate, and he likes her."

"What will you give me in return?" Clearly, Seb had learned much from his master, who made his living trading, after all.

"Three of our kittens. Miriam can keep Abigail, and Ta-Muit would have a mate. You will have three more cats to take home with you."

"Do your mother and I have any say in your plan?" Father asked him. His left eyebrow was raised, but he looked amused.

"It's a good plan," Joel answered. "We love all the kittens, but there are too many of them."

"And there will be more," Father added. "Ta-Muit will soon be ready."

"We can give them away after they're born."

"To whom?"

"Issachar will take one. And I bet Benjamin would want one."

Father looked at Seb. "What do you say, lad? Is it a good trade?"

"Three cats for one? Yes, it is good."

"And will your master agree?"

Seb nodded. "He will no doubt trade or sell them in the next town. Failing that, we will bring them back to Egypt."

"And do you want to return there?" Father asked.

Seb did not answer.

"Does your master beat you?"

The boy shrugged. "Not often. I am learning more and more how to please him."

Then Father surprised Joel. "Would you like to stay here, in Jerusalem?"

"Nathan—" Mother began.

What is Father thinking? Joel wondered. *Let Seb stay here? I would have a brother?*

Seb did not have to think long. "No, thank you. You are kind to offer, but Egypt is my home. One day, I will be a man, and I will make my fortune away from the one who calls himself my master."

Father nodded his agreement.

"And will you make the trade?" Joel asked.

"Yes," Seb agreed.

"Then we will make sure your master accepts it, as well."

Seb said goodbye to the gray Persian named Rustum. Miriam said goodbye to Kush, Jacob, and Esau. She hated to let them go, but she felt better when Father promised that with Rustum in the house, there would be more babies before she knew it.

Father and Joel went with Seb back to the market. The Egyptian was delighted with the bargain Seb had struck, and he praised his sharp business sense. Father took the man aside and talked earnestly to him. Joel guessed he was repeating what he had said the last time they met, how YAH did not care for men who harmed children, and YAH was always watching over the widow and the orphan to see that they were protected.

Joel said goodbye to the three kittens, and like his sister, he felt a pang of sadness. He wished them well, and he felt assured that they would be cared for, because everyone knew how the Egyptians doted on their cats. These three from Israel would find welcoming homes.

As Joel walked with his father back toward their house, he had much on his mind. Suddenly, raucous cries overhead interrupted his thoughts. He looked up and spied three white birds winging their way north. No flocks had flown overhead for many days, and these were stragglers. But they flew fast and strong, and they would surely be reunited with their companions soon enough.

The sight of the three together made him smile, but now he didn't long to join them—not just yet. Jerusalem was home. He had found favor with the king, and he had received permission to use his gifts in ways he'd never thought possible. His parents loved him, and he had walked safely through the gate between the world of childhood into the world of grown men. There was much for which to be thankful, but at the moment, two things stood out above all the others:

Ta-Muit.

And soon, there would be many, many cats in Jerusalem.

www.ingramcontent.com/pod-product-compliance
Lightning Source LLC
Chambersburg PA
CBHW070617310726
48982CB00001B/104

* 9 7 8 1 6 6 6 7 2 7 9 8 2 *